OMINOUS

OMINOUS

A PRIVATE NOVEL

KATE BRIAN

SIMON AND SCHUSTER

First published in Great Britain in 2011 by Simon and Schuster UK Ltd
A CBS COMPANY

Originally published in the USA in 2011 by Simon Pulse,
an imprint of Simon & Schuster Children's Division, New York.

alloy**entertainment**

Produced by Alloy Entertainment
151 West 26th Street, New York, NY 10001

Simon & Schuster UK Ltd
1st Floor, 222 Gray's Inn Road, London WC1X 8HB

A CIP catalogue record for this book is available from the British Library.

ISBN 978-0-85707-149-1

1 3 5 7 9 10 8 6 4 2

Printed in the UK by CPI Cox & Wyman, Reading, Berkshire RG1 8EX

www.simonandschuster.co.uk

For Mom, who's my biggest fan

OMINOUS

WASTE OF TIME

I couldn't move. Outside Billings Chapel, the wind howled. The ancient floorboards overhead creaked and groaned. My bones were like ice. I stared down at the title of the book in front of me, hardly able to absorb what I was seeing.

THE BOOK OF SPELLS.

This could not be real. I wasn't actually standing in the basement of a centuries-old chapel faced with a dusty, leather-bound spell book. I felt like I'd just stepped into a Nancy Drew novel and taken over as the heroine. Tentatively, I reached out to touch the cover, but before I could, the book was snatched away.

"You *have* to be kidding me," Noelle Lange blurted out, holding up the heavy book. Her dark, windblown hair was fanned out over her shoulders and her face was red with fury. "This is why she sent us here? A *spell book*?"

My heart caught as she waved the antique tome around like it was no more valuable than an out-of-print dictionary. "Noelle—"

"You know what I'm going to do with this, Grandmother?" she shouted at the book. "I am going to track you down wherever you are right now and smack you upside the head with it!"

"Noelle, just . . . calm down. Don't go psycho on me now."

She hesitated but threw the book back down onto the podium, tossing up a cloud of dust that filled my nostrils. I coughed painfully.

"Oh, *I'm* the psycho?" Noelle said sarcastically, yanking her cashmere scarf from her neck with shaking hands. "Right. Because *I'm* the one who sent us out here in the middle of the night in a snowstorm to find an old book!"

She threw the scarf over the back of a chair and unbuttoned her wool coat. Apparently her anger was making her hot.

I walked over to the podium and opened the book, and all the air went out of my lungs. There, in handwriting I'd recognize anywhere, were the words *Property of the Billings Literary Society*.

Elizabeth Williams had been a student at the Billings School for Girls back in 1915. I had spent so much time poring over her writings in the Billings Literary Society book, I could probably copy her script by now. I felt like I'd gotten to know her since reorganizing her secret society at Easton Academy. I knew what colors she liked to wear, how she was fiercely loyal to her friends, how she loved living away from home. But now I felt as if I didn't know her at all. Because nowhere in the BLS book had she ever mentioned a word about spells, or witchcraft, or this huge volume we'd just discovered. Not one single word.

Noelle stormed over to my side and nudged me out of the way. She opened the book to the center—to a page titled "The Purity Spell"—then quickly flipped the pages forward and back.

"What're you doing?" I asked.

"Checking to see if it's one of those hide-a-key book things," she said. "You know, with a big chunk cut out to hide something that actually matters?" She heaved a sigh and slammed the book closed. "Nope. Nothing. Unbelievable."

She started across the room, grabbing her scarf again as she went, coiling the ends around both hands and pulling it taut. "You coming?"

"Where?"

"Back to campus," she said impatiently. "Personally, I don't feel like wasting any more of my time up here."

"You're not gonna take this with you?" I asked, gesturing at the book.

She rolled her eyes and popped one hip. "Do I *look* like Sabrina the Teenage Witch?"

I clucked my tongue. "No, but your grandmother . . . our grandmother . . . ," I said hesitantly. I'd only just found out that Noelle and I were half sisters—that her dad was my biological father—and the words weren't exactly rolling off my tongue. "She wanted us to find it. Maybe there's more to it than you think. Maybe there's . . . I don't know . . . something in there she wants us to read."

"Fine then." She slid the book off the podium and started for the stairs. "Happy now?"

"Ecstatic," I said sarcastically.

I followed her up the winding stairs toward the deserted chaplain's office above, a sparsely decorated room that hadn't been used for dozens of years. Noelle muttered something under her breath, clearly annoyed, but as we closed the bookcase door behind us, my heart pounded with curiosity and longing. I wanted to know what was in that book—to know what it had to do with Elizabeth Williams.

Noelle yanked open the office door, and we both heard a tentative creak coming from inside the chapel. We froze and I grabbed her forearm. That had sounded a lot like a footstep. It was after midnight. Why would anyone be up here? Noelle looked over her shoulder at me, eyes wide, and I attempted to swallow.

"Hello?" she called out.

There was no answer. Outside, the wind whistled through the bare branches of the forest.

"Is someone out there?" I shouted. All I could see was a darkened sliver of the chapel that contained a random pillow on the floor where someone had left it after the last BLS meeting, a folded blanket, half the preacher's pulpit, and an empty LUNA Bar wrapper.

Another creak. I gasped. Noelle set her jaw and stepped out into the chapel, dragging me with her.

"No!" I blurted out, terrified.

"Come on," Noelle said, letting out a sigh. "Let's get the hell out of here."

She walked purposefully down the center aisle, me scurrying along with her. The wind forced squeals and cracks and groans from the ancient wood walls. I didn't breathe again until we were out-side the chapel, gasping in the crisp winter air, and the door had slammed behind us.

"I swear I'm going to kill that old crone," Noelle said, jamming her wool hat down over her brow.

"Let's just get back to campus," I said, eyeing the book. "And don't drop that, okay? There's snow and mud everywhere."

Noelle rolled her eyes and hugged the book to her chest. "I'll guard it with my life," she said mockingly.

Another loud creak sounded from inside the chapel, and I jumped.

"Race ya?" I said.

"Okay," she replied.

And we both took off, half speed walking, half jogging through the forest, trying to make ourselves believe there was nothing to fear.

BIRTHRIGHT

The following morning, I took the stairs to Noelle's single in Pemberly Hall. My eyes were puffy and at half-mast—I hadn't slept at all. I'd spent the entire night thinking about my mom and dad, Noelle's father, our grandmother, Elizabeth Williams, and that crazy book—and wondering why I couldn't just worry about normal things. Like my grades. The SATs. My college applications. Those were the things every other junior in the country was worrying about. I couldn't help but wish I'd never left Croton, Pennsylvania.

I knocked on her door. It took Noelle a moment to answer, and when she did, she grabbed my arm and pulled me inside.

"Wait. Reed just got here," she said into her iPhone. "I'm putting you on speaker."

Noelle placed the flat cell phone atop her dresser and stepped back. She wore a gray wool skirt that came halfway down her calves, paired with heeled black boots and a black ballet-neck sweater. Her dark brown hair was pulled back from her face on the sides, and her makeup was impeccably done, complete with fully lined eyes and lavender eye shadow.

Apparently *she* had slept. I pulled my navy cotton cardigan tighter around my wrinkled long-sleeved T-shirt and stifled a yawn.

"Girls?" Mrs. Lange's voice came through the speaker loud and clear. "Girls, are you there?"

"We're right here, Grandmother," Noelle said, placing her hands on her hips.

"Reed?"

Noelle knocked me with her elbow.

"I'm here," I croaked.

"Good. Noelle is a bit . . . out of sorts this morning," Mrs. Lange said, sounding displeased. "Perhaps you can help me calm her down."

"Calm me down?" Noelle blurted. "Like that's gonna happen. You sent us out into the snow in the middle of the night to find the quote-unquote *key to our future* and what do we find? A book about witchcraft." She went over to her bed and yanked the thick tome out from under a tangle of bedsheets and silk pajamas, holding it up as if her grandmother could see it. "Is that what you're trying to tell us, Gram? Really? That you think we're witches? I'm sorry, but you're either senile or really, *really* bored."

I took the book from Noelle with two hands, tired of watching her fling it around like an old paperback novel. This book had once belonged to Elizabeth Williams and was therefore a precious relic to me—whether or not the content was ridiculous.

"Seriously, Grandmother, have you ever thought about taking up mah-jongg?" Noelle continued without pause. "I hear it really helps keep your faculties in order."

"Noelle," I scolded under my breath.

She widened her eyes at me. "*What*?"

Through the speaker, I heard Mrs. Lange take a deep, patient breath. "Girls today are so skeptical and jaded. But you two—you have no idea the power you could wield."

Noelle rolled her eyes.

"So . . . ?" I said slowly, hugging the book to my chest. "Are you saying that *you've* actually done witchcraft?"

"No," she admitted. Noelle threw up her hands and turned away. She'd been back at school for almost two weeks and her Louis Vuitton rolling case was still open on the floor. She picked it up and turned it over, dumping its entire contents out on her gold and burgundy throw rug. "No one at Billings has practiced in a long time," Mrs. Lange continued. "But the two of you . . . Girls, you have no idea how powerful you could be, now that you're together."

I felt an odd chill go through me, and I looked over at Noelle. She was sorting through a pile of balled-up sweaters, crumpled socks, and tangled necklaces, her fingers shaking slightly.

"You have a unique opportunity here," Mrs. Lange continued, oblivious to Noelle's silent tantrum. "You might be able to fix certain things, set right the unpleasant . . . situation that has arisen at Easton."

Noelle stood up straight, her arms falling down at her sides, one hand clutching an Hermès scarf, the other the gold chain strap on a Gucci purse. We looked at one another, and I knew we were thinking the same thing: The woman *was* senile. But then I saw a flash of movement behind Noelle, a blur of color against the stark white snow outside. Stepping over the pile of clothes at my feet, I carefully walked to the frost-laced window and peered out. There, across the quad at the decimated site of the former Billings House—our former home— was a group of people in long wool coats. I recognized the perfect posture of Headmaster Hathaway and the jet-black curls of Demetria Rosewell, one of the more powerful Billings alums. They walked carefully around the jagged stone outline that was the footprint of the demolished building, along with a pair of men who pointed and jotted notes on clipboards and bent their heads together in the bright sunshine.

I felt a familiar hollowing-out sensation in my gut. "What's that about?" I whispered to Noelle.

"I don't know," Noelle replied, coming up behind me.

Chilling words, coming from her, since normally she knew everything. Although lately, my know-it-all friend had dropped the ball more than once. The idea of her not always being in charge was going to take some getting used to. I turned and looked at the phone.

"Mrs. Lange?"

"Yes, Reed."

"Do you mean . . ." I kept one eye on the group out the window, their feet sinking into the snow. "Do you mean that we might be able to bring Billings back?"

For the first time that morning, Noelle looked intrigued.

"Now you're thinking, Reed."

There was a glimmer of pride in her voice, and I felt it in my chest. I'd made my grandmother proud. Weird. Noelle and I looked at each other, then out the window. Mrs. Rosewell was shaking hands with Mr. Hathaway, nodding in a satisfied way. The sunlight glinted off Mr. Hathaway's wide smile. There was something foreboding about it. Like someone was making a deal with the devil, but I wasn't sure which side was good and which was evil. All I knew was that I didn't like it.

Noelle and I exchanged a glance. What if we *could* bring Billings back? Wouldn't it be worth it to hear our grandmother out?

"No. No way." Noelle shook her head and stepped away from the window, as if she was shaking herself out of a daydream. She tossed her things onto her bed. "We are *not* witches, Grandmother. This is not some CW summer series."

"I don't know what that means," Mrs. Lange said.

"It means this conversation is over," Noelle replied. She plucked the phone off the dresser and held it in front of her mouth. "I'll call you later, Grandmother. We're late for breakfast." Then she ended the call before Mrs. Lange could protest.

"Well," I said. "That was rude."

"She'll get over it," Noelle replied, shoving the phone into the rust-colored Birkin bag she was currently using for her schoolwork. She turned and sat down on the mound of her comforter with a sigh. Her shoulders slumped slightly. "I'm sorry, Reed." She looked up at me tentatively. "For everything. The whole faked-kidnapping thing was her idea. She kept talking about birthright and us being sisters and how you needed to go through this test to prove that I mattered more to you than anything. . . . She said if you passed, then we'd have our reward. I thought it was just another one of her eccentric projects to pass the time and figured she was going to . . . I don't know . . . give us the keys to some villa in Spain I'd never heard about so we could bond this summer." She sighed again and her eyes fell on the book, which I still held clutched to my chest. "I never would have said yes to any of it if I knew she was batshit crazy."

"It's okay," I said, releasing my grip slightly so I could look down at the worn cover. "I can see how she could be really . . . persuasive."

A tingling sensation sprang to life in my chest and traveled down my arms and into my fingertips, making the book feel warm in my hands. I never would have said this to Noelle in a billion years, but there was this teeny-tiny part of me that wondered . . . what if Mrs. Lange *wasn't* crazy? What if what she'd said was true and we could wield some kind of power? I'd seen some insane stuff since I'd started school at Easton last fall. Nothing supernatural, of course, but definitely crazy—things I never would have thought were possible even two years ago. What if this was possible too?

"Okay, forget this."

Noelle plucked the book right out of my hands and tossed it back onto the mess of her bed. My fingers felt cold suddenly, and I tucked them under my arms.

"I say we concentrate on more important things," she said, her brown eyes bright.

"Like what?" I said, trying not to look over her shoulder at the book.

"Things based in actual reality." She reached for her black-and-white plaid coat and opened the door for me, but I hesitated. "What?" she asked impatiently.

"Do you mind if I take that?" I said, gesturing toward the book. "I mean, if you're not going to look at it—"

"Seriously?" She walked to her bed, picked up the book, and held it out to me. "It smells like rotting garbage and mold. *Please* take it."

I reached for the book, but she snatched it back toward her shoulder, giving me an appraising glance. "As long as you promise me you're not going to try anything in it. Because I really don't think I could be friends with someone who actually believes in this crap."

I held her gaze. "I promise."

Her eyes narrowed further, but after a long moment she handed the book over. I stuck it in my messenger bag and pulled the flap down over it.

"As I was *saying*," Noelle said as we stepped out into the hallway. "I think we should talk about throwing you the most kick-ass seventeenth birthday party in the history of birthdays. You're a Lange now. I'd say you're well overdue."

Instantly, my shoulder muscles coiled.

"I'm not a Lange."

I tried to keep the irritation out of my voice, but it didn't entirely work. The thing was, I barely even knew Noelle's dad, and I wasn't even sure if I wanted to. But I was certain that I didn't feel like part of their family. I was a Brennan, and I always would be.

Noelle rolled her eyes as she started to close the door behind us. "Whatever. Daddy did call you, right? He said he left you a message."

"Yeah. He did. I just . . . haven't gotten around to calling him back yet," I told her.

I'd gotten the message yesterday morning, right after I'd left the hotel where Mrs. Lange had given us the key and sent us on our wild-goose chase. My mother and I had hit a diner for lunch and had just sat down in our booth when the phone rang—an unrecognizable 212 number. Later, after listening to the message, I'd lied to my mother and told her it was my boyfriend, Josh. Because how was I supposed to tell her that the guy who'd fathered me all those years ago was now calling me up, saying he wanted to be a part of my life? She'd chosen my dad. Chosen to forget her mistake and leave my biological father behind. And now . . . because of me . . . he was back.

So as of this moment, I had no intention of returning his call.

"Actually, Noelle, I wanted to talk to you about that. . . . Can we keep this whole sisters thing between us for now? If that's okay with you," I added quickly.

She froze with her hand on the doorknob. "Why?"

"I just . . . I don't want to deal with all the questions and explanations and everything until I'm a little more used to it," I said.

"Wow. I would think you'd be kinda psyched to be my sister," Noelle said. Only she would have a big enough ego to say something like that without a hint of irony or self-deprecation.

"It's not that," I told her. "It's just . . . it's kind of humiliating, you know? I'm going to have to tell everyone that my mom cheated on my dad with your dad." I looked at my water-stained leather boots, mottled after days of tromping around campus in the snow and sleet. "There's no getting around that."

Noelle's expression changed utterly. It was pretty clear she'd never thought of the whole thing from my perspective before. "Yeah. Okay. I get it." She closed the door with a bang. "But you still deserve a party."

She had me there. Given that she'd faked her own kidnapping, scared me to death, and made me jump through multiple hoops to find her over the past couple of weeks—I'd say I deserved whatever good things she wanted to throw my way. A party might be just what the psychoanalyst ordered after everything I'd been through recently.

Her eyes flicked over me as if she was noticing my outfit for the first time and did not approve. "Where's your coat?" she asked.

I glanced down at my jeans. "Oh. I guess I forgot it."

She shook her head, walked back inside, and came out two seconds later with a stark white wool trench. "See? You should *definitely* be psyched to have me as a big sister. I'm already taking care of you."

"Thanks," I said with a smile, slipping my arms into the sleeves of the expensive coat. She'd always taken care of me, and we both knew it. Until that last little escapade of hers, anyway.

She closed the door, took a big breath, and blew it out. "Okay. Let's start with location and date. I'm thinking the city, on your actual birthday, since it falls on a Friday. Unless you've got some better plans back in Bumblefart, P.A."

I tried not to bristle at her insult to my hometown. I'd gotten used to it over the past couple of years, but somehow, now that she was of the opinion that I'd never belonged there, what with the Lange blood in my veins, it felt more personal. I might not have loved my hometown, but it was my home. And I did love my family, including my father, who would always be my dad, no matter what.

"No," I said. "No plans. I think a party in New York would be perfect. But it's only a week away. Can you really pull something together that fast?"

She ducked her chin. "Try to remember who you're talking to."

"Right. Silly me."

As we walked down the hallway toward the stairwell, I felt the weight of the book knocking against my hip over and over again, and I itched to steal back to my room and open it up—check out those notes Elizabeth Williams had written in the margins, see if I recognized any of the other handwriting. Maybe I'd have a chance to do it later, when Noelle wasn't around. Because even though I didn't believe in spells, I was sure she would tell me I was ridiculous for caring about these girls who had lived almost a hundred years ago.

But I did. And I was dying to know more about them.

IRONY

"So you bailed from school for two weeks so you could go to some *spa* in Sedona?" Portia Ahronian said, lifting her fur-lined hood over her head as we walked toward the chapel after breakfast. She tucked her thick black hair inside the hood, untangling some strands that had gotten caught up in one of her many gold necklaces. "What about all your homework? And your tests?"

"Hathaway had them e-mailed to me," Noelle lied casually, lifting a shoulder. "When your father helps the headmaster land his job, he tends not to say no to you."

"And why, exactly, did you have to scare the bejesus out of us the night you left?" Astrid Chou asked, popping some contraband cereal from her hand into her mouth. She dusted the sugar from her hands, then slipped on her colorful yarn gloves, which she had attached to the sleeves of her purple coat with kiddie-style glove savers—an accessory only quirky Astrid could get away with on an upscale campus like

Easton. "I honestly think Amberly almost had a coronary, and as the only one among us who knows CPR, I was not about to go there."

"Hey!" Amberly Carmichael protested, her pert pink lips twisted into a pout. "You wouldn't save my life?"

Astrid shook her black bangs off her face. "*Maybe*. But only if you promised me that red Chloé bag of yours."

My friends laughed and I could tell none of them were really still angry with Noelle for the prank she'd pulled on the night of her "disappearance." Everyone was just glad to have her back, safe and sound. Of course, I hadn't had a chance to tell her that I'd told Ivy Slade she was actually at home with her mom, but that was a flub that could easily be glossed over if Ivy started asking questions.

"Sorry about that, guys," Noelle said, returning to the subject as our feet crunched over the salted stone walk. "I was just messing with Reed. I owed her one, and you guys just got stuck in the middle. But I promise—no more drama for the rest of the semester."

"Great. You just jinxed us," Kiki Rosen said, pausing on the third step of the Easton chapel and turning around to look at the rest of us. A stiff breeze kicked up her hair, half of which she'd recently dyed neon green. "We are *so* screwed."

Noelle rolled her eyes but smiled as Astrid hooked her arm through Kiki's and dragged her inside. Together, the two of them looked like a colorful tear sheet from a comic book. I swallowed back a lump of foreboding as I watched them disappear. Kiki was right. Around Easton, no one should ever promise a lack of drama. It was like tempting the fates.

"Speaking of the chapel, Reed, when's the next meeting of the BLS?" Tiffany Goulbourne asked quietly. She'd been bringing up the rear, scrolling through some photos on her camera with Rose Sakowitz. Tiffany was never without her camera, even though with her perfect warm brown skin, almost six-foot frame, and athletic body, she could have definitely been posing in *front* of one rather than shooting from behind one. She whipped out her BlackBerry as she approached, ready to type the meeting into her calendar. Tiffany had always been one of my more responsible friends, but unlike the rest of them, she seemed to be getting *more* organized the closer she got to graduation, instead of less. The other seniors had slowly started to slack, copying homework assignments or faking migraines to get out of class. But not Tiffany.

"We're in need of some girl bonding," Rose added, looking a little pale beneath her mass of red curls.

"Um . . . honestly, I hadn't really thought about it." I looked off across campus toward the woods around Easton, where the Billings Chapel stood. Suddenly, I itched to skip morning chapel and dash over there. I wanted to check the place out, see if there was anything Noelle and I had missed last night—any more clues to what Elizabeth Williams and her friends had been doing with a book of spells almost a hundred years ago.

Ironic, considering that just a couple of days ago I'd been seriously pondering the idea of never coming back to this place. After Noelle had faked her own kidnapping, I'd all but decided I wouldn't be returning to Easton Academy this semester. I was done with all the insanity, the selfishness, the entitlement. But then Mrs. Lange had explained that the whole thing had been her idea, and had lured me back here with all this mystery and talk of what was to come, and I'd fallen for it like a satellite plummeting back to Earth.

"Why don't we do it tonight?" I suggested. "I'll send out a text later."

"A text about what?"

Josh appeared over Tiffany's shoulder and her eyes bulged out like she was afraid we'd just been caught. What Tiffany didn't know was I'd already confided in Josh about our secret society—back when he'd been trying to help me figure out who'd snatched Noelle. She and Rose didn't need to know that, though. I didn't want them thinking I'd betrayed their trust just because Noelle had taken a spa sabbatical.

"Nothing you need to worry your pretty little head about," I joked, pulling him toward me. We touched noses and I smiled, inhaling that very particular Josh scent of evergreen soap and dried paint.

"I missed you," he said.

"I missed you, too," I replied.

"Ugh. Let's go inside before we catch whatever cheesy grossness has sickened these two," Noelle joked.

She and the other girls jogged up the marble steps as Josh and I kissed hello. He opened his coat and wrapped it around me along with his arms, nestling us together in a warm Josh and Reed cocoon. As I cuddled against him and deepened the kiss, I wondered how I ever could have imagined leaving here—leaving him. Next year, Josh would be off to college and we'd hardly ever see each other.

"We need to do something. Go somewhere," Josh said quietly,

pulling back. He lifted one hand and gently brushed his fingertips across my cheek. "How long has it been since we've gone on a date?"

I narrowed my eyes, pretending to think. "Since forever?"

"All right, then. With your permission, I'll make a plan," he said, touching his forehead to mine. "ASAP."

"ASAP sounds good," I replied.

"What the hell is she doing here?" Josh said suddenly.

My eyes popped open and I turned around. Headmaster Hathaway strode toward us from the direction of Hull Hall with Demetria Rosewell in tow. My first thought was, *Double H is going to miss morning services*. But I realized in the next second that this was not the pertinent fact here. Nor was Demetria the "she" to whom Josh had referred. Striding along behind them was Paige Ryan—the daughter of the person who had recently tried to murder me multiple times in St. Barths. Josh shot her a scowl as she walked by, but all she did was grin. A few steps past the chapel, she paused and looked behind her.

"Missy! Are you coming or not?" she asked.

Missy Thurber, my worst nemesis at Easton, jumped away from Constance Talbot and London Simmons and scurried after her cousin Paige. She also gave me a grin as she hurried by, but hers held a lot more meaning. It said, *I know something you don't know*.

My heart sank inside my chest, and I looked back at Constance and London. The two of them turned and hustled inside, avoiding my eyes.

"What was that all about?" Josh asked, entwining his fingers with mine.

"I don't know," I replied. "And I don't think I want to know."

NO DRAMA

"I love the idea of a party to honor the seniors," I told Amberly that night as we kicked back on the floor of the Billings Chapel. "Do you want to put a committee together?"

"Yes! I'd *love* a committee!" Amberly said, clapping her hands.

I could see a few of the girls wince at the idea of being roped in by Amberly and toiling under her direction, but it was her idea, so they'd just have to deal. We'd just been finishing up our meeting when Amberly had very formally presented a "piece of new business" as if we were at a board meeting, rather than sprawled out on silk pillows, chenille blankets, and fur throws in a deserted chapel. Rose had provided the refreshments tonight—gourmet cupcakes shipped in from New York City—and there were crumbs, sprinkles, and coconut shreds everywhere. Vienna Clark groaned, her hand across her flat stomach, a bit of chocolate stuck to the corner of her mouth.

"Okay, if there are no *other* new points of business," I said, "then I'd say we're adjourned!"

The convivial chatter started up as soon as the words were out of my mouth, and my friends began to gather up their things. Noelle clasped Vienna's hands and hoisted her off the floor, while Amberly practically jumped Lorna Gross and Astrid, asking them to join her committee.

"You ready?" Ivy asked, lifting her long black hair out of her red coat and letting it fall down her back.

"Actually, I think I'm going to hang back for a little while," I said, gesturing over my shoulder in what I hoped was a casual way. I had a plan for the evening, and it did not involve going back to campus.

Noelle paused near the door and cocked an eyebrow. I glanced away nervously. Maybe my gesture hadn't hit the mark. "I don't want to leave all these crumbs. We could attract mice."

"Oh. Then I'll help," Ivy said.

She started to put her bag down again and I panicked. "No!" I blurted.

Both Ivy and Noelle were staring at me now with matching expressions of concern and confusion. Which was interesting, considering how much they hated each other. Noelle crossed her arms over her chest.

"It's just . . . I kind of want to be alone," I said. "I've got a lot to think about and I . . . I guess I've never told you guys this, but I like to clean while I think. It helps me relax."

Ivy's brow crease deepened, and for a moment I thought she would put up a fight, but then Noelle turned, gently knocking Ivy with her shoulder. "Come on. Let's leave the freak to her cleaning therapy."

If anyone knew I really *did* have a lot to think about, it was Noelle. Apparently she was taking pity on me. Which kind of made me feel guilty about all the lying. Bad Reed.

"Okay," Ivy said slowly. "But I don't *love* the idea of you being out here alone."

"I'll be fine," I promised her. "I've got my phone if I need anything."

The two of them finally capitulated and followed after the others outside, everyone waving and shouting their good-byes as they slipped out into the night. When their voices had finally died away on the wind, I took a deep breath and looked around. Except for the few flickering candles, the chapel was dark. Some of the stained glass windows had been broken long ago, leaving behind jagged, incomplete mosaics, the stars winking outside their busted panes. The pews were polished and buffed—thanks to the members of my secret society—and the wood floors were swept clean, but high in the rafters there were still some heavy cobwebs and a stray bird's nest.

Quickly blowing out all but one candle, I slipped my arms into Noelle's white coat to guard against the chill of the basement, grabbed my messenger bag and the last candle, and walked to the office at the back of the building.

I placed my candle in the holder on the dust-covered desk, then walked to the bookcase on the west wall. Using both hands, I pried the bookcase away from the plaster. It swung open, letting out a silence-splitting creak of protest. Behind it was the smaller, white paneled door with its brass knob and an old-fashioned keyhole. I tugged the key on its purple cord out of the pocket of my jeans. As I slid the key into the hole, I glanced back over my shoulder to make sure none of my friends had returned. Then I turned the key with a click, and the ice-cold doorknob turned easily in my grasp.

Frigid air rushed up from the basement, along with a musty yet somehow cozy smell that made me think of the basement of the Croton library. The dank room housed all the historical books, and older kids were always getting caught making out down there. I reached back for my candle and held it high in front of me as I descended the stairs, feeling a rush of excitement. I'd been looking forward to this moment all day long.

When my foot hit the concrete floor, I paused. My throat was dry as I looked around. The basement room was a perfect circle. Eleven chairs were set up to face the center, and at that center was the podium, plain and sturdy and made of wood. I walked around the room until I was positioned against the wall directly behind the rostrum. Then I whipped the skirt of Noelle's coat into my lap to keep from soiling it, and sat.

Inhaling a bit of the musty air, I looked slowly around the room and smiled. Elizabeth Williams had hung out here. She'd been in this very room with Theresa Billings and Catherine White and all the other girls mentioned in the BLS book. I wished I knew what they looked like, and wondered why I'd never thought to try to dig up photographs of them before. They'd had cameras in 1915, hadn't they? Tomorrow

I would have to check the Easton archives and see if I could find any photographs.

I tugged out the BLS book first and opened it to the second page, where each of the members of the first Billings Literary Society had signed their names. Then I slowly opened the book of spells. Near the front was a list of basic spells, and next to each was a little tick, as if someone had checked them off after completing them. Next to some items there were notes, written in a few different hands:

Third attempt successful, or *Must be done with two sisters, holding hands.*

Some of these notes were in the same slanting script as the BLS book—there was the curled-down tail on the *y*'s and the flourish on the *s*'s. That small scroll to the *w*'s, *m*'s, and *n*'s. The handwriting belonged to Elizabeth Williams.

Carefully, I studied some of the other notes, my eyes flicking back and forth from the signature page in the BLS book to the book of spells. Suddenly, my heart caught. Some of the other notes had been written by Catherine White, Elizabeth's best friend. Her lowercase *a*'s and *o*'s were perfectly rounded, almost like a child's handwriting.

A shiver of satisfaction went through me, like when I figured out a calculus problem. I paged through the book of spells, glancing at some of the titles. The Forgetfulness Spell. The Swelling Tongue. Spell to Mend a Broken Heart. Then something caught my eye as I whipped past, and I slowly paged back. Written across the top of the page were the words *The Presence in Mind Spell*.

That handwriting was not Elizabeth's, but it looked familiar. I glanced back at the list of signatures and picked it out right away. The strokes were thick and confident, the uppercase letters overly large. The spell had been written out by Theresa Billings.

"This is so freaking cool," I whispered.

I looked around the room again, hugging myself against the cold. I imagined Theresa, Elizabeth, and Catherine at the podium, jotting down notes in the book. Had they really cast spells in this room? Had any of them worked? Was that even possible? Or was it a game to occupy their time?

Biting my lip, I flipped to the incantation near the front of the book of spells—the one that could supposedly turn a group of eleven regular girls into witches. I'd found it that afternoon at lunch, when I'd spent the period holed up in a study carrel at the back of the library. The directions were explicit. Eleven girls dressed in white were required. They were to stand in a circle, each holding a candle, and recite the incantation. A thrill of silly excitement went through me. If it required eleven girls in white to work, then it couldn't do any harm for me to say it on my own, could it?

"Like it could do any harm anyway, loser," I whispered to myself. "This stuff isn't real."

I took a deep breath and held it, squelching an embarrassed giggle. Then I moved my candle over the page and read.

"We come together to form this blessed circle, pure of heart, free of mind. From this night on we are bonded, we are sisters." My voice shook with giddy mirth at my own childishness, but whatever. This was fun. "We swear to honor this bond above all else. Blood to blood, ashes to ashes, sister to sister, we make this sacred vow."

I heard a creak that stopped my heart, and suddenly a gust of wind shot through the circular room, swirling my hair up off my shoulders and extinguishing my candle. Heart in my throat, I scrambled to my feet, the books tumbling to the floor at my toes. The acrid, birthday-party smell of the candle's smoke curled through my nostrils as heavy footsteps clomped down the stairs, every groan of the ancient planks like an arrow to my heart, every crack heightening my terror. I pressed my back against the wall, wondering if there was any way to use my candle as a weapon. Then, suddenly, out of nowhere, the candle flickered to life again. I stared at the flame, transfixed, my heart seized with fear.

How could that have possibly happened?

Just then, Noelle arrived at the foot of the stairs. Her hands braced the walls, level with her ears, and she looked at me with a wry expression.

"I knew it!"

"Noelle! You scared the crap out of me!" I blurted.

"Which you deserve!" she said, tromping across the room. "What are you doing? Please tell me you're not really taking this stuff seriously."

She wrested the BLS book from my hands and looked at it. "What are you, writing a term paper now?"

I grabbed the book back and, with a trembling hand, shoved the freaky candle at her. As I crouched on the floor, cramming the books into my messenger bag, I took a few breaths to steady myself. Obviously the wind had gusted down the stairs when Noelle had opened the door. And as for the candle . . . it was just a faulty wick. Or one of those trick candles that could relight itself.

Except I'd never seen one of those that wasn't birthday-cake-candle size.

"I was just messing around," I improvised, shouldering my bag as I stood. "I was trying to figure out whether those Billings Literary Society girls really believed in this witchcraft crap."

Noelle, to my surprise, looked interested. "And? Did they?"

"Some of them, I think," I said, lifting my shoulders. For some reason, I didn't want to name names. I felt like I'd be betraying the BLS girls somehow. Opening them up to Noelle's ridicule. Which was, of course, ludicrous, since all of them had been dead for probably thirty years.

"Yeah, well, people were a lot more gullible back then," Noelle said, turning and heading for the open doorway. "Come on. There's still a mess upstairs and I am *not* hanging out here again if it's infested with mice."

"I'm right behind you," I told her, keeping an eye on the candle, which she held up in front of her. She started up the steps, but I paused at the bottom, glancing around the room one last time.

It's just a room, I told myself. *Just like every other room at Easton.*

I lifted my foot and placed it on the first stair, and as I did I felt a light breeze against my face. I looked around. There were no openings in the stone wall. No windows anywhere, being that I was below-ground. Shrugging it off, I kept walking, but at the third step, I felt it again. And by the fifth it was stronger. By the seventh it was stronger still, the wind right in my face, slowing my progress. By the tenth step, the flame of the candle in Noelle's hands had died, and by the twelfth, I had to squint my eyes to see. When I got to the top, I slammed the door behind me, breathless.

"Since when is that staircase a wind tunnel?" I asked.

Noelle's carefully brushed hair stuck out from behind her ears, and some of her bangs stood up straight on her forehead.

"Must be that window," Noelle said, gesturing at the pane behind the desk. The top was completely bare, as if someone had broken it, removed all the shards, and never replaced it. My insides squirmed as I stared at the bending and swaying branches of the trees outside.

"I don't remember that being broken before," I said.

"Well, it is now," she replied casually. "Come on. Let's clean up and get back to Pemberly. We need to talk guest list for your party."

"Okay."

I tried to sound as excited as she did, but as we walked out I took one last trembling look at the window, half expecting to see Elizabeth Williams's ghost reaching out to me. I closed the door firmly behind me and jogged to catch up with Noelle.

If I really wanted a life with no drama, maybe it was time I stopped walking around in the middle of the night looking for it.

ELIZABETH

"Billings will only live on in you, Reed. You're the only one who can set things right."

My breath was a white cloud in front of my face. Stars twinkled merrily through the tangle of branches overhead. I stood in the center of a small clearing in the Easton woods, wearing nothing but my Penn State T-shirt and mesh Easton Soccer shorts.

"Billings must live on, Reed. The book of spells is real."

Someone was speaking, but no one was there. The voice sent a warm, familiar tingle down my spine, but not from fear. It was almost as if I recognized the delicate tones. Like I'd heard them somewhere before.

"It's real, and I can show you proof."

A sudden movement in the corner of my vision stopped my heart. A young girl, about my age, stepped out of the trees. It was as if she'd materialized out of nowhere, out of the ether, but she wasn't a ghost.

She looked solid and real and three-dimensional as she slowly, deliberately crossed the forest floor. She wore an old-fashioned dress with a blue plaid skirt and a darker blue wool jacket, the hood pulled up to cover her dark brown hair. Her eyes were green, kind of like my mother's, and as she approached I realized she was almost my height, though far slimmer. I could have placed my hands around her tiny waist and I was sure my fingertips would have touched. She came within two feet of me, but I didn't flinch. There was nothing threatening in her.

"You're very beautiful," she said, tilting her head to one side. Her lips moved, but her voice didn't issue from her throat. It came from all around, as if the trees held hidden surround-sound speakers. "But it's not the most striking thing about you."

"What is?" I asked.

She smiled slowly. "Oh, I think you know. And if you don't, you will soon enough."

"Who are you?" I asked.

"I think you know that, too."

She turned with a smirk and walked over to the edge of the clearing. Elizabeth Williams. It had to be. What other specter would my subconscious conjure up for me? Because clearly that's what this was—a dream. Otherwise, how had I gotten here, to the center of the Easton woods? At the foot of an ancient oak tree, she crouched, her skirts billowing before they floated to rest on the ground. Behind her, at a slight distance, the spire of the Billings Chapel hovered above the topmost limbs of the bare trees, its face stark white against the night sky.

"Here," she said, touching her suede-gloved fingertips to the dirt. It was untouched by the snow, canopied as it was by a web of thick branches. *"Here is where we buried the books and promised never to speak of them again."* She looked up with a wry but sad smile. *"Of course, promises are made to be broken."*

"Books?" I asked. "There was more than one?"

She nodded slowly, looking at the ground. She trailed her fingers reverently—almost lovingly—back and forth, as if she were remembering something or someone she cared for deeply.

"Yes. The others have long since gone missing. Scattered on the four winds to places unknown." Then she looked me in the eye. *"But the book of spells, the most vital of the books, that's in safe hands now."*

I knelt down across from her. Although I could still see my breath and there were goose bumps visible on my skin, I didn't feel the cold at all anymore. Nor did I feel hot. It was as if I were somewhere outside my body, and nothing that touched it mattered.

"Why are we here?" I asked.

"Because you are a skeptical girl, Reed Brennan. You need proof." She lifted her hands and clasped them atop her knees. *"I've come to tell you how to find it."*

She said this last bit in an excited tone, as if she were a little girl proposing a new scheme. I was about to answer when my eyes flicked past her shoulder. Something had just moved, there in the trees. A figure. A girl. I was sure of it. But when I stared into the darkness broken by tree trunks and underbrush, I saw nothing.

"Tomorrow night, you will return to this place," Elizabeth instructed.

"Bring a shovel, and a candle to light your way. If you dig in this very spot, you will find what you are looking for."

A shock of blond hair ducked behind one of the trees. My heart skipped and I stood up. A branch cracked. I caught a whiff of a scent—something earthy and sour—and my senses recoiled. It smelled like death. Leaves rustled. The sounds grew closer. There was someone out there. Someone moving toward us through the trees. I opened my mouth to warn Elizabeth, but suddenly my throat constricted. It was as if someone had curled their fingers around my throat and started to squeeze, but no one was there. When I tried to call out, all that I could manage was a croak.

I waved both my hands, trying to get Elizabeth's attention, but her head was bent toward the earth. She was stroking the ground with her fingertips again. Behind her, the branches swayed. The crunch of footsteps approaching grew louder still, but she didn't flinch. Didn't look up. There was no air, and I couldn't move. Not to defend her, not to defend myself.

Suddenly someone sprang from the underbrush and pounced on top of Elizabeth, wrestling her to the ground. A blur of blond hair and pale skin. The girl closed her fingers around Elizabeth's neck, slammed her head into the dirt floor of the forest, and whipped her head around to glare over her shoulder at me.

"Ariana!"

My door banged open and I sat up straight in bed, my hand covering my heart. Ivy stood in the doorway, her hair knotted with sleep, her nightshirt falling off one shoulder. She held an aluminum softball bat over her shoulder.

"Reed! Are you all right?"

She pulled the bat back and looked quickly around the room, as if ready to destroy the first thing that moved.

"Why?" I asked, trying to catch my breath.

Her stance relaxed slightly. "Because you were just screaming about Ariana."

My cheeks warmed with embarrassment. But the memory of what had just happened in my dream was burned on my brain. Elizabeth Williams had been dying at the hands of Ariana Osgood. It was all so impossible, but it had seemed so real. I remembered exactly where we had been when Ariana had attacked. Just north of the Billings Chapel, at an untouched clearing in the woods.

I glanced at Ivy's concerned face as she lowered her bat to the floor.

"It was just a dream," I said.

She sat down at the foot of my bed. "Not a good one, from the sound of it."

My heart still pounded fretfully. "Yeah. No."

"What was it?" Ivy asked, shifting slightly. "Do you remember?"

I chewed on the inside of my cheek, drawing my knees up under my chin. I wanted to tell her about it before the details slipped from my mind. Tell her about the clearing and the spot Elizabeth had indicated. She'd probably tell me it was just a dream—that I was crazy. Which would probably be a good thing. Because would a sane person actually be considering following a dead dream-girl's orders?

"Ivy, there's something I need to tell you," I said seriously. "It's about the BLS."

Ivy placed the bat aside, leaning it up against the sliver of wall between the end of my bed and my closet.

"Okay," she said, matching her tone to my own. "I'm listening."

PARTICULARLY JOSH

Josh had looked at me like I was crazy more than once in our year-and-a-half-long on-and-off relationship, but never for so long, or with such complete conviction. We sat at our private table in the corner of the dining hall, while the rest of Easton Academy laughed and chowed down and checked over homework around us.

"What?" I said finally, turning my spoon upside down to suck strawberry yogurt off of it.

Clearing his throat, Josh shimmied forward on his chair, shoved his tray of half-eaten turkey sandwich aside, rested his elbows on the table, and leveled a dubious stare at me. One dark blond curl fell over his forehead and I smiled slightly, feeling that little tingle I felt whenever something particularly Josh happened—something only I would know was particularly Josh.

"So let me get this straight," he said. "After everything that's happened on this campus—the murder, the stalking, the kidnapping—you want to go up into the woods—by yourself, in the middle of the night, based on something a ghost in a dream told you—and dig a hole?"

Well, when he put it that way . . .

"Come on. I basically *have* to do it," I said, placing the spoon and yogurt cup down. "If I don't, I'll *always* wonder if there was really something there."

It was Ivy who had convinced me. That morning, as I'd gotten dressed, I'd railed on about how it was only a dream. And you didn't see me running around Croton, Pennsylvania, looking for a river made of marshmallow fluff, did you? (That was a recurring dream of mine when I was in kindergarten.) No. You didn't. Because dreams are complete insanity conjured up by our subconscious, not treasure maps to be followed in the dead of night. Ivy had listened to all of this patiently before saying the magic words—the ones I had just repeated to Josh.

"Yeah, but if you don't go," she'd said, her arms crossed over her chest, "you'll always wonder."

"Can I ask you something?" Josh said, dusting some cookie crumbs from the corner of his mouth. "What time did you have this little nightmare?"

I narrowed my eyes, wondering why that could possibly matter. "Um . . . it was this morning. When I woke up the sun was up. Like . . . six thirty?"

Josh's green eyes widened. He picked up another cookie. "That is *so* weird."

"What?" I asked.

"I had a nightmare this morning too, and you were in it," he said. "I don't remember what it was about, exactly, but when I woke up I looked at the clock and it was exactly six thirty-two."

I felt an eerie tingle all down my back and froze with my spoon halfway to my mouth. "Really?"

He smirked and popped the cookie into his mouth. "No."

"Ugh." I balled up my white linen napkin and chucked it at him. He ducked to the side and the napkin fell innocently to the hardwood floor behind him.

"Okay, about this plan of yours, can I just say . . . no?" Josh said. He used his napkin to wipe his mouth, then tossed it down and chugged a glass full of whole milk.

"No?" I asked incredulously. "Since when do you tell me what I can and can't do?"

Josh laughed, pulling his head back and shaking it in an amused way. "Like I'd ever try. No. I wasn't telling you *no*, you couldn't go. I was telling you *no*, you're not going alone." He paused and wiped his mouth with the napkin again, this time clearing away a milk moustache. "I'll be coming with you. As of now, I'm not letting you out of my sight for one second."

"Oh," I said, feeling silly.

"Unless you think 'Elizabeth' would mind," he added, throwing in some air quotes.

I laughed and rolled my eyes at him. "I don't think she'd mind at all."

PROOF

The snow on the quad was frozen solid across the top, so that the crust would hold for a moment with each step before the crunchy layer gave way and my boot sank into the softer, wet snow beneath. Every now and again, if I stepped just lightly enough, I left no footprint at all. My trail appeared as though I had played a sporadic game of hopscotch: a two-footed jump here, a one-footed hop there. The moon shone down on campus, reflecting off the otherwise smooth snow, brightening the sky and giving almost the illusion of day.

As I approached the landscapers' storage building on the outskirts of campus, everything was still. No night owls, no crickets, not a living thing stupid enough to be out and about and making noise. Not one except for me. And . . .

"Josh?" I whispered harshly, creeping around the corner of the building, which bordered the woods. "Josh, are you—?"

A crash loud enough to wake the dead stopped me in my tracks.

I briefly considered bolting, but then the side door slowly creaked open and Josh poked his head out—along with the heads of two rather large shovels.

"Sorry. Did I scare you?" he asked.

"Me and half of Connecticut," I said, glancing back at the darkened windows of Hull Hall, my hand over my heart.

"You know, when I suggested going on a date, this is not what I had in mind," Josh said, stepping outside.

"I know. We're still going to do that," I promised him. I looked at the open padlock on the shed door. "So how did you—"

"Hey!"

Josh and I both screamed and clutched each other, the business end of one of the shovels nearly colliding with my skull. I released his arm when I saw Ivy trudging toward us. She wore a black ankle-length coat and a black skullcap, and she had her hair done in two thick braids.

"What are you doing out here?" I demanded.

"You didn't really think I was going to let you guys do this without me, did you?" she asked, raising her perfectly thin eyebrows. She lifted her chin toward the shed. "You should probably relock that."

"Don't you want a shovel?" Josh asked, angling toward the door.

She scrunched her nose. "I don't do shovels."

Josh laughed. I wished Ivy had told me she was coming instead of startling us in the middle of the mission, but I was glad to have her along. Sneaking around the eerie Easton woods in search of a ghost's legacy was definitely a "the more the merrier" type of situation. Josh secured the lock on the door, slung both shovels over one shoulder, and nodded toward the woods.

"Lead the way, Elizawannabe," he said.

I shoved him lightly and started into the woods. The spot where I'd been standing in my dream faced the back of the chapel, so I decided to walk around to the back, then head north from there to try to find the clearing. The three of us walked along in a straight line, Josh behind me and Ivy behind him, the woods silent except for the crunching of our shoes and the hiss of our breathing. Suddenly I remembered playing jungle adventures with my brother, Scott, and his friends when we were little—tromping through the woods behind our middle school with toy canteens and flashlights. Only then, my pulse hadn't been pounding in my ears in this annoyingly unnerving way.

"Wow," Josh whispered as we stepped into the large clearing around the chapel. "That's a beautiful church."

"You've seen it before, right?" I said, glancing over my shoulder at him.

He'd paused near the cornerstone and tipped his head all the way back to better see the tip-top of the spire. "Yeah, but never at night. I should come back up here and paint it before graduation."

My heart panged at the thought of Josh leaving Easton, and he seemed to notice the change in my expression. He reached for my gloved hand and squeezed it.

"Which is many, many weeks away," he reminded me.

I nodded. Ivy hung back at a respectful distance, her hands in the pockets of her coat, but I couldn't help remembering that not that long ago, it would have been her hand he was reaching for. It was awkward enough when she'd been dating him and he was my ex, but now I was dating him again and he was *her* ex. The very fact that the three of us could be in the same room together, let alone on the same mission, was a small miracle. I cleared my throat and pulled away.

"Come on. We're almost there."

I walked to the center of the back wall, then turned my steps perpendicular to it and headed straight toward the woods. Now that we were so close, I suddenly realized how completely futile and insane this whole endeavor was. What did I really think I was going to find out here? This was just a product of my overactive imagination, spurred on by my obsession with the BLS and the book of spells.

But when I got to the tree line, I paused. Right in front of me was a pathway. It was a bit grown over, but it was there.

"What's up?" Josh asked, coming up behind me.

"Look." I pointed at the ground, trailing my finger up to indicate the line of the path. We both squinted into the darkness. Up ahead, it looked as if the trees parted. "Is that—?"

"A clearing?" Ivy said, stopping at my opposite shoulder. "You bet your ass it is."

She pushed ahead, leading the way into the woods.

"I suppose we have to follow her," Josh said.

"It would be rude, right? To leave her here alone," I joked back.

"Majorly."

I glanced up at the sky for a moment, feeling suddenly that someone was watching. Not in a bad or scary way, just in an . . . interested way. I reached for Josh's hand, glad that I didn't have to do this alone, and lifted my foot to step over the pile of dead leaves at my feet. When we caught up to Ivy, she was standing in the center of a circle of trees. The ground beneath her feet was packed dirt, no snow in sight. My heart quivered. I couldn't have *sworn* it was the exact same clearing from my dream, but it was familiar. Slowly, I trailed my eyes around at the trees—oaks and birches, evergreens and maples. And then I froze.

"What?" Ivy and Josh said as one. "What is it?"

Josh sidestepped closer to me, the shovels clanging together, as if trying to see whatever I was seeing from exactly my vantage point.

"There," I said, pointing. "That's it. That's the tree from my dream."

Ivy and I arrived at the foot of the enormous oak at the exact same time. She crouched down, just as Elizabeth had the night before, and I was hit with a sickening punch to the gut. I almost reached out to grab her—to pull her back. But then, that was ridiculous. It wasn't as if Ariana was really about to charge out of the woods and attack.

I took a deep breath to calm my fluttering heart and studied the woods around us. There was no one there.

"Look at this," Ivy said. "This area is packed down in a whole different way. Look. It's lower than the rest of the clearing."

My stomach filled with butterflies the size of baseballs. Josh swung the shovels off his shoulder and handed one to me. He drove the tip of his straight into the hard, cold dirt.

"What are you doing?" I asked, stopping his arm with my hand.

"Digging," he replied, matter-of-factly. "Isn't that what we came here to do?"

I smirked. "What happened to skeptical Josh?"

"He's officially left the building," Josh replied. "So are you gonna help me or what?"

The two of us started to dig, while Ivy tucked her coat beneath her legs and sat down on a wide, exposed tree root to watch. The ground, frozen solid, made the work slow and frustrating. Every now and then a hard jab with the shovel would yield only half an inch of silt. Still, every second I envisioned myself hitting pay dirt—imagined the point of my shovel hitting something hard and metallic—whatever it was Elizabeth Williams had supposedly sent me here to find. At some point clouds moved across the moon, darkening the woods around us, and Ivy had to flick on the two flashlights she'd grabbed from the emergency kit in our dorm. Soon my shoulders started to ache and my abs got tired of supporting my back. I wiped sweat from my brow, wondering when I'd gone from freezing to overheated.

"Reed?" Josh said. He leaned both hands atop the end of his shovel handle and looked up at me. He was standing in a ditch about four feet deep. There was a streak of dirt from his nose to his earlobe. "Can we stop now?"

I glanced at Ivy. She was shivering in the cold. "How long have we been doing this?"

"Two hours," she said, without glancing at her watch. She sighed. "This sucks."

"I know. I thought for sure we'd find something," I said as Josh clawed his way out of the hole. "Maybe," I added, realizing how nutso I sounded. But then, they were here with me, and they hadn't even had the dream.

"Are you sure you've never been in this clearing before?" he asked, taking a deep breath. "Maybe you dreamed about it because you've seen it yourself, not because—"

"Not because the ghost of Elizabeth Williams wanted me to find it?" It sounded beyond ridiculous, even to me. I couldn't believe I'd led two of my best friends up here for nothing. "I'm so sorry, you guys. I feel like a complete—"

Just then, the clouds overhead parted, sending several shafts of moonlight down through the branches of the trees. Out of the corner of my eye, I saw something glint. Right in the center of one of the piles of dirt Josh and I had produced around the hole.

"Ivy! Shine one of the flashlights over there!"

"Where?" she asked, standing up at the urgency in my voice.

"There!" I pointed at a spot just to the left of Josh's feet, between him and the trunk of the tree. Ivy did as she was told, and I lost all ability to breathe.

"Oh my God," Ivy and I said at once.

Josh whirled around as if he expected Elizabeth to jump down from the tree and bite his neck. I quickly skirted the hole and dropped to my knees next to the hint of gold. Using my aching fingers, I pushed the dirt aside until I'd uncovered a large, round pendant. I tugged it out by its chain and let the pendant lie flat in my palm. It was warm to the touch—odd, since it had been buried in frozen earth for who knew how long. An intricate design had been etched into the surface, and I tried to clear the grime away with my fingernail so I could make it out.

"What is it?" Josh asked, hovering over me.

Slowly I stood and polished the tarnished gold on my jacket. Finally I cleared enough of the dirt away to make out the design in the moonlight. Suddenly my head went light, and I reached out to grab Josh's shoulder for support.

"What?" Josh asked again. "What is it?"

"It's the same design," I said, turning quickly to show it to Ivy.

Ivy brought her face low, her eyes hovering just over the swirling circle motif. "Exactly the same," she said.

"Will someone please tell me what's going on here?" Josh asked.

I looked up at him, my eyes shining even as my heart pounded with uncertainty and fear. "It's the same design that's etched into the cover of the book of spells."

THE BOMB

"So now you're so desperate for good jewelry you'll just wear any old thing you find in the dirt?" Noelle said as she sat down in her usual seat at the Billings table: last on the end, facing the door so she could see everyone coming and going. "If you really want something, I'm sure Daddy will get you whatever it is. He's still waiting for you to call him back, by the way."

I rolled my eyes and dropped my tray across from hers. The locket felt warm against my skin and it gleamed in the overhead lights, thanks to the vat of jewelry cleaner Ivy had soaked it in overnight.

"That's all you have to say?" I asked, fingering the locket as I sat. "I tell you that the ghost of a Billings Girl led me to a necklace in the woods near the chapel, and all you can do is insult me?"

Noelle flicked her napkin into her lap and shook salt and pepper onto her sliced hard-boiled egg. One of the crystal shakers clinked against her gold ring. She hadn't looked me in the eye in about five minutes.

"Noelle—"

"Reed, do you even hear yourself?" she asked finally, resting both wrists on the edge of the table. "You sound like a crazy person. You don't want to tell anyone that we're sisters, but you're perfectly fine running around telling everyone that some dead person led you to a locket in the woods?"

My heart panged with some unidentifiable emotion and I touched the locket again. Just then Tiffany and Portia slid past us to sit in the next two chairs. Noelle shot me a warning look, clearly telling me to keep my mouth shut, as if I needed to be told. She was the only one I was interested in talking to about this.

"Wait until you see the centerpieces I designed for your party," Noelle said, deftly switching to a more audience-friendly topic. "I'm going with a whole Pisces theme, and I found a guy who does floral centerpieces with tiny aquariums in the bottom of the vases. Real fish and everything."

"Fabulous," Portia said, lifting her hair over her shoulder.

"What do they do with the fish after the party?" Tiffany asked.

"Don't get your La Perlas in a twist, green girl. Daddy's going to take them all home for his personal collection," Noelle said. She tore off a piece of her bagel and popped it into her mouth, looking at me mischievously. "He's paying for the whole thing, you know."

A huge rock formed between my heart and my throat, and my hand automatically went to the locket again. I suddenly became very interested in my cereal.

"Really? That's nice of him," Tiffany said, eyeing me curiously.

"Why would he do that?" Portia asked, lifting her fork. "No offense."

I shrugged and gave them a tight smile.

"He just knows how very close Reed and I are," Noelle said, spearing an egg slice. "I mean, we're practically sisters."

I choked on my orange juice and a little bit of it went up my nose.

"All right, Reed?" Noelle prompted.

"Yeah. Sure."

I managed another smile and took a deep breath, trying not to cough again.

"Reed! What an amazing locket," Portia said suddenly, reaching for the pendant, which I hadn't realized I was still toying with. "It's so . . . unique." She ran her thumb over the surface. "Definitely an antique. Where did you get it?"

I shot Noelle a panicked look. "Um, I got it at a rummage sale when I was home."

Portia scrunched her nose. "What's a rummage sale?"

"Would you let go of her already, P?" Noelle demanded. "She's turning blue."

Portia released me and I sat up straight again, righting the locket and rubbing at the back of my neck where the chain had cut into my skin. Portia was still sizing up the necklace out of the corner of her eye as she took a bite of her fruit salad.

"You should have that appraised. It could be worth something," she said.

I glanced at Noelle, feeling hot under my arms and around my collar. "Yeah," I said. "Maybe I will."

Kiki and Astrid arrived, dropping into the chairs next to Tiffany and Portia. Then Lorna, Amberly, and Vienna crowded into the last few seats, adjusting their trays on the table so everything fit.

"Check this out," Astrid said, lifting her chin toward the head table where the headmaster and the tenured teachers usually sat. My blood turned cold when I saw that Mr. Hathaway was holding out a chair near the head of the table for Demetria Rosewell. She wore a winter white suit that made her black hair stand out even from across the room. She shook her curls back as she sat and gave a thin-lipped smile as the headmaster introduced the teachers around her.

"Why has she been hovering so much lately?" I said under my breath.

"I can tell you why."

A chill shot down my back as Missy Thurber leaned toward me from behind. She rested one hand on the back of my chair and the other on the corner of the table. She must have been walking down the aisle behind me when I'd posed my question. She smelled of lavender perfume and peanut butter—a gag-inducing combination—and I held my breath. Constance and London hovered at the end of the table. From the corner of my eye I saw Sawyer Hathaway, my friend and the headmaster's son, stand up from his table. He had a worried look on his boyishly handsome face, like he was anticipating a fight.

"I don't think anyone here was talking to you, Missy," Noelle snapped.

Missy stood up straight, mercifully giving me room to breathe, and moved to stand next to her friends. Lifting her chin so that I could practically see her brain through her huge nostrils, she addressed the entire table with the air of a girl who knew she was about to drop a serious bomb.

"Demetria Rosewell and Paige Ryan have decided to donate a few million dollars to the school to have Billings House rebuilt," she said snidely.

My heart skipped an excited beat. Billings was going to be rebuilt?

"Why do I have a feeling that's not everything?" Noelle asked, lowering her fork.

"Well, Demetria has been convening with the board the past few nights, coming up with a list of requirements for admission to the dorm," Missy said. "But they've already decided on one thing." She turned and looked me in the eye. "You, Reed, won't be getting in. Not after all the trouble you've caused this year."

My heart dropped and my fingers curled into fists atop the table.

"In fact, *none* of you will be in," Missy said, making sure to look each of the others directly in the eye. "The board asked me for a list of the girls who were the most disruptive influences during all that mess with Cheyenne and Sabine last semester, and I was more than happy to provide it."

"Missy," Lorna said from the far end of the table, "you didn't."

Missy's cruel eyes slid over to her former best friend. "You chose your side. Now I've chosen mine." Her mouth twisted into a wide grin. "Ta, ladies!" she said, twiddling her fingers at us. Then she turned on her heel and strode off. Constance shot me an uncertain look, ducked her head, and followed, with London behind her.

"This. Cannot. Be happening," Amberly said loudly.

I looked across the table at Noelle, whose face was so red I thought she might start to melt. Then suddenly Sawyer was there, looking sheepish with his hands in the pockets of his slim-cut gray cords. He wore a white shirt open over a black band T-shirt.

"Hey," he said tentatively. "Are you okay?"

"Is it true?" I said, looking up at him through my lashes.

Sawyer gritted his teeth. "Yeah. I'm sorry. I would've told you, but I only found out this morning."

"Why?" Noelle asked. "Why would your father go to them instead of my dad?"

Sawyer turned a little green, and I could tell that whatever he had to say next, he was afraid of saying it.

"*They* came to *him*," he said. "And when they did, my dad called your father to check . . . to make sure he didn't want to try to outbid them or something. See, Dad didn't want Billings back at all, but apparently the school needs the money so . . . I guess he figured whoever would donate the most could control the project."

"He told you this?" Tiffany asked.

"No. I overheard him this morning." He turned to Noelle. "On the phone with your dad."

"And?" Noelle and I said at the same time.

Sawyer closed his eyes for a moment, as if gathering his strength. "He said no. He said he didn't want to have anything more to do with

Billings, and he didn't want his girls anywhere near it either."

My face burned and my eyes met Noelle's across the table.

"His *girls*? WTF?" Portia said. "Have you got some secret sister we don't know about, Noelle?"

The other girls laughed halfheartedly, but I felt the orange juice traveling back up my throat. This—all of it—was very not good.

"Obviously, Sawyer misheard," Noelle said through her teeth, staring me down. "And don't worry, ladies," she added, lifting her hair over her shoulders. "I'll get to the bottom of this. There's no way I'm leaving Billings in the hands of a loser like Missy Thurber."

DATE NIGHT

"Sorry I couldn't get us passes off campus," Josh said. He dimmed the lights to a romantic glow and sat down across from me at the small pedestal table he'd placed in the center of the art cemetery. Arranged on its small wooden surface were boxes of steaming Thai food, everything from lemongrass chicken to coconut rice to salmon with mango sauce. "After everything that's gone on in the last year, I guess Hathaway's finally cracking down."

I smirked as I reached for the chopsticks. "Or he just hates both of us."

"That too," Josh conceded. He lifted his wineglass full of sparkling champagne. "Still, I think I did pretty well."

I picked up my glass and clinked it with his. "I'll second that."

We looked into each other's eyes as we sipped our faux champagne, and I felt a twist of anticipation. When it came down to it, the art cemetery was the best place we could possibly be. Because all I could think about was kissing him, and kissing him in a way that probably couldn't be done in a public forum.

"You want to forget the food?" Josh asked suddenly.

I dropped my glass on the table with a clang. "Good plan."

We both stood up and collided with each other, his lips on mine before I could even catch my breath. He cupped my face with both his hands and tripped us sideways into the old-fashioned love seat pressed up against the wall. My feet hit a set of gilt-framed paintings as I fell on top of Josh, knocking the whole stack over with a terrific clatter, but neither of us even paused. I fumbled my hand up under Josh's sweater and was met with the rough fabric of his chambray shirt.

I pulled away, my lips buzzing. "Can you?"

"What? Oh yeah."

He sat up to tear his sweater off and I sat back to give him room. As he flung it on the floor, I went right to work on his buttons until I saw a hint of his bare chest, and then I kissed it. He leaned back again as I kissed my way over his collarbone, up his neck to his ear, and then found his mouth again. He let out a little moan as he kicked off his shoes. Then he shifted sideways, kind of tossing me aside so that we were lying facing each other, my back against the back of the couch.

I felt like we hadn't been alone together in weeks, even though it was only days, and from the frantic direction of Josh's hands, I could tell he felt the same way. It was like he wanted to touch every inch of me as quickly as possible, all the while kissing my lips. He pulled back suddenly and looked directly into my eyes. It took a moment for me to catch my breath. My hand was inside the opening of his shirt, holding onto his waist.

"I love you, you know," he said, trailing a fingertip down my cheekbone.

"I love you too," I said.

Then he laid his palm flat on my cheek. His fingers were unbelievably warm and his breath was ragged on my face. "But we're not gonna do this here."

I looked up into his eyes. "We're not?"

He leaned in and kissed my cheek, then my temple, then my forehead. "We're going to do this, don't get me wrong. Just not . . . here."

I swallowed a lump that had formed in my throat and exhaled. My head dropped forward and I rested my face against his chest. He placed his chin atop my head and just held me. He was right, of course. We couldn't have our first time together be here. In this place where Dash McCafferty and I had confronted Thomas Pearson's brother, Blake, after Thomas had died. This place where Sabine had drugged Josh and tricked him into hooking up with Cheyenne. It had always been our place before that, and we'd made it our place again since. But it was tainted. And Josh and I—we deserved better.

"Are you mad?" he asked.

"No," I replied, shaking my head as best I could.

"Will a present make it better?" he asked.

I lifted my chin to look up at him. "Always," I said with a laugh.

He sat up and I did too, adjusting the skirt of my dress, which had ridden up a considerable amount. Josh took a deep breath and blew it out, like he was relieved to have gotten through that conversation. I smiled and put my hand on his back. For some reason, in that moment, I loved him more than I could have imagined possible.

Glancing at me over his shoulder, Josh leaned forward and tugged something out from under the couch. It was a dark gray book with weathered yellow pages. When he placed it on his lap, I could just make out a gold date embossed near the bottom right corner.

1915–1916

My heart all but stopped "Is that—?"

"The Billings School for Girls annual," he said, holding it up so I could see the spine. "Complete with class photos."

"Shut. Up!" I said, grabbing for the book. He held it away—over the arm of the couch—like we were suddenly playing one-on-one out on the basketball court. "Where did you get that?"

"I dug it out of the archives this afternoon."

I got on my knees and made another grab, but his arm was annoyingly long. He lifted his other hand to stop me and my butt hit the cushions again.

"What?" I asked petulantly.

"You have to promise me one thing," he said.

"A gift with provisions? I don't like it," I joked.

He smiled and placed the book in my hands but kept his own heavy palm on the cover, holding it closed. "If she looks different in the picture than she did in your dream, you'll drop this," he said. "No more midnight treks through the woods, no more listening to people who appear in your dreams. Promise me you'll drop it."

I looked at him, the words crowding my throat, but I couldn't seem to let them go. His green eyes turned serious and he looked at the floor. "Reed, I just . . . I want you safe, okay? That's all."

"I know," I said. "I get it."

And I did. Because after everything, that was all I wanted from him, too.

"I promise. If she looks different, I will drop it," I told him.

"Okay," he said. He lifted his hand from the cover.

I hesitated, looking at him uncertainly. "Josh? What if she *does* look the same?"

His eyes clouded with concern. "Then . . . I don't know." He nodded at the book. "Page twenty-two."

I hungrily skipped to the designated page, rushing by ancient print and grainy black-and-white photographs. When the book fell open to page twenty-two, I stopped. Because there, staring back at me from a sepia-toned photograph set in a large oval, was Elizabeth Williams. The dark hair, pulled back from her face. The creamy white skin. The almond-shaped eyes. Her expression was serious, more serious than I would have predicted. There was a slight smile on her lips, but sorrow in her eyes. Eyes that I knew would have been green if the photo were in color.

Because Elizabeth Williams was the girl from my dream.

Tentatively I touched my fingertips to the page, feeling the depth of her sorrow within my chest. Beneath the photo was the inscription

ELIZABETH JUNE WILLIAMS and below that, one word, ELIZA. So she'd really been called Eliza. I liked it a lot more than Elizabeth. It was less stuffy somehow.

"The thing is . . . ," Josh said slowly, putting his arm behind me on the couch, pressing his hand into the cushions near my hip. "The thing is . . . she looks like you. A *lot* like you."

"Really?" I said, tearing my eyes from the photograph.

Whatever Josh saw in my eyes made him blink. "It's her, isn't it?"

"Yeah," I said. "It's her."

His Adam's apple bobbed as we both looked down at the picture again. "Reed. I have to tell you something."

"What?" I asked, breathless.

"The other day, when I said I had a nightmare and you were in it? And that I woke up from it the same time you woke up from yours?" he said.

I pressed my tongue into the top of my mouth. "Yeah?"

"That wasn't a joke," he said. "I actually did have that dream. I just . . . didn't want to freak you out."

My head went light and fuzzy and it took a moment for me to focus. "What was the dream about?"

Josh slumped back into the couch and pressed the heels of his hands into his eye sockets. "I don't remember. I know you were in trouble. I think someone was . . . trying to kill you."

My heart dropped to my toes as his hands dropped from his eyes.

"You screamed to me for help, and then I woke up."

I breathed in and out, trying to normalize my body. Trying to stop the rushing blood, the screaming thoughts, the terror and—oddly—the excitement that seized my heart at once. I turned my head and stared down at Eliza Williams, silently begging her to tell me what it all meant.

"Okay. That's . . . okay," I heard myself say slowly.

Josh sat forward again and looked me in the eye. "What the hell's going on, Reed?"

I touched the locket around my neck, the metal suddenly so warm it reddened my fingertips. "I wish I knew."

NOT WITCHES

"She really does look like you," Ivy confirmed, looking from the open yearbook to me, then back down again. We were sitting in the center of my dorm room, her with the BLS book and me with the book of spells, comparing the two and trying to figure out which dates in the BLS book corresponded with which spells. It was amazing how careful Eliza had been. Nowhere in the BLS book did it mention spells or witchcraft or anything other than regular old meetings, gatherings, parties, and community service projects that the secret society had done. "You have the same jawline. And the eyes . . . Do you think you could be related?"

"Yeah, right," I said.

Because that's what the old me would have said. The one who was a product of two no-names from Pennsylvania. But now that I knew I was a Lange, who knew where the hell I'd come from—who my ancestors might be? Still, Noelle had never mentioned being related to

Eliza Williams before. She would have claimed that connection if it was there, wouldn't she? I took the book from Ivy, closed it, and set it aside on the floor. She went back to studying the BLS book and I went back to the book of spells.

"Did you notice there are some pages missing from this?" Ivy asked, turning the book toward me on the floor. I leaned forward to see the spot she'd opened to and, sure enough, there were a few jagged tears down the center of the book. Carefully, I ran a fingertip over their edges, feeling a shivery sense of apprehension.

"How did I not notice that before?" I asked.

"I don't know. You've practically been living this book," Ivy said. She shrugged and lifted it back onto her lap. "Whatever it was, it was written by Eliza. Her handwriting's on the pages before and after," she said, lifting her shoulders again. "Guess it was something she didn't want anyone to read."

I slumped back against the side of my bed, feeling—ridiculously—betrayed. "Yeah. I guess not."

Slowly I flipped back to the front of the book of spells. The first page was a careful, intricate drawing of intersecting circles. I ran my fingertips over the design, thinking of Eliza and wondering what she'd felt the first time she'd seen this book. Touching my fingertips to the locket—which, as always, felt warm against my skin—I turned to the next page: The Initiation Rite. I felt a flutter inside my chest, recalling what had happened when I'd read the rite on Friday. I looked up at Ivy tentatively. She was staring right at me.

"What's up?" she asked.

I licked my lips. "What if we recited this incantation?"

She looked at me, her face a blank slate. "Why, exactly, would we do that?"

"I don't know." I lifted a shoulder. "For fun."

She gave a thoughtful frown, then shrugged. "Okay."

She closed the BLS book and set it aside, angling for a better look at the book in my lap. One thing I loved about Ivy Slade: She was always up for anything.

I laughed. "That's it? Just 'okay'?"

She looked at me with a wry smile. "Why not? Nothing's going to happen."

I tilted my head, hoping she was right. She had to be right. Because even if I believed that Eliza Williams had actually visited me in a dream, and even if I thought it was weird that the gold locket always felt warm, and even if my candle had gone out then relit itself, it wasn't possible that magic actually existed. It just wasn't possible.

"We need candles," I said.

"Why? You need to make this charade official?" Ivy joked. But there was something serious behind her eyes. Maybe she was more freaked by my finding the locket in the woods, and by the fact that Eliza really had been in my dream, than she'd let on.

"Okay. Forget it," I said, disappointed.

Ivy scooted over next to me and crossed her legs so that our knees were touching. I moved the book so that it laid across both our laps, half on my thigh, half on hers. "Okay. Ready?" I said. She nodded and we began to read.

"We come together to form this blessed circle. . . ."

Both of us paused, looking at each other. We weren't exactly a circle.

"Let's hold hands," Ivy suggested. She pulled her hands out from under the book and we clasped our fingers together over the pages. "Okay. Start again."

"We come together to form this blessed circle, pure of heart, free of mind. From this night on we are bonded, we are sisters." I looked at Ivy here and we both smiled goofily. "We swear to honor this bond above all else. Blood to blood, ashes to ashes, sister to sister, we make this sacred vow."

That was when the lights went out.

"Holy shit," Ivy said under her breath.

I sucked in some air, still clinging to Ivy's hands. It was just like the other night when my candle had died. Then both our cell phones rang at the exact same time, their tiny screens lighting up to cast square beams from the floor to the ceiling. I let out a noise that was half gasp, half squeak.

"Okay. Okay. Calm down," Ivy said, gripping my fingers so hard they hurt.

She released one of my hands and grappled for her phone. "It says 'unknown caller,'" she said, staring down at the screen, which cast a glow over only half her face.

I swallowed hard and grabbed my iPhone. My throat went dry. "Mine too."

Then both screens went dead in our hands. "Ivy. There's something I have to tell you," I said in the darkness, my breath shallow and quick. My whole body prickled with sweat. "The other night, I said the incantation by myself in the basement at the chapel. And when I did, there was this sudden wind, and my candle went out, and two seconds later, it relit."

"And you didn't think to tell me this *before* we said the stupid thing together?" she hissed.

The door to my room opened suddenly, and Ivy and I both screamed. Noelle took one look at us and leaned into the side of the doorway. She was backlit by the hall light, which meant that only the electricity in my room had died. She held a tri-folded letter.

"What the hell is this?" she asked.

Then her eyes flicked to the book of spells, which had fallen off Ivy's lap, but still laid halfway on mine. Yeah. I was never going to live this one down.

"Are you kidding me?" she said, standing up straight. "You guys! We are *not* witches!" she hissed, glancing over her shoulder into the hall.

Ivy and I looked at each other, my right hand still clinging to her left. Noelle hadn't seen what we'd just seen. And even though her sudden, larger-than-life presence had brought me somewhat back to reality, the niggling belief I'd started to have when Josh showed me Eliza's picture the night before was starting to grow.

Maybe . . . Was it possible? Could we be witches?

The moment the thought occurred to me, I laughed out loud. Because how ridiculous was that?

"We were just messing around," Ivy said, dropping my hand and standing up. She wiped her palms on the back of her jeans and rolled her head around, cracking her neck. Her dark ponytail swung down her back and I took a deep breath at the sudden normalcy. Even my skin was starting to cool down.

"Good." Noelle hit my light switch and the overhead lights popped on. I looked up at them, startled. "Because *I* have something to show you guys," Noelle said, taking a couple of steps into the room. She turned the page around, holding it in both hands to show us. "I just got into Yale!"

"Are you serious?" I blurted out, jumping up. I grabbed the letter from her fingers and read the first couple of lines. "Noelle! Congratulations!"

Throwing my arms around her, I hugged her hard. Tears sprang to my eyes as it hit me full force that she would be gone next year, for real this time, but I told myself this wasn't about me. Yale was what Noelle had always wanted. She'd be at school with her boyfriend, Dash McCafferty, and the two of them would surely be the power couple on campus. Plus, New Haven wasn't that far from Easton. As Ivy League schools went, it was the best possible outcome for me.

"That's great, Noelle. Congratulations," Ivy said as I released Noelle. She even managed to sound sincere. "Did you call Dash?"

"Of course. I expect a huge box of Yale crap in the morning," Noelle said with a giddy laugh. "But right now, we party."

"What?" I asked, glancing at the clock. It was already past ten.

"You heard me. We're going to the chapel. Get your crap together, bitches," Noelle said. "It's time to celebrate."

ALIVE AND WELL

Kiki cranked up the sound on her new iDock as the rest of us danced in a circle with Noelle at the center. She threw her arms up over her head and swung her heavy hair around, dancing for all the world as if there was no one around but her. It wasn't like Noelle to let loose to quite this degree, but then, she'd finally secured her future and she deserved this celebration.

Plus, she'd already downed an entire bottle of Taittinger on her own. So I'd also never seen her quite so drunk.

"Go, Noelle! Go, Yale! Go, Noelle! Go, Yale!" Amberly chanted along with Lorna and Rose, their fists pumping in the air. Vienna swigged from a champagne bottle with one hand, recording the party on her Flip with the other. She was swaying a bit in her high-heeled Ferragamo boots, and I could only imagine the tape was going to be nauseating to watch. All I could do was hope the whole thing wouldn't end up on Facebook later that night.

Noelle bent at the waist, then flipped back up again, trying to execute some kind of sexy move, but she fell backward instead. She tripped into my and Ivy's arms but quickly righted herself and cleared her throat.

"Tiffany's turn!" she shouted, tossing her hands up, then grabbing Tiffany and dragging her into the center of the circle.

Tiffany blushed but obliged, doing a few hip-swinging moves in the middle before whipping out her camera and clicking off some random shots of the rest of us. That afternoon, she'd also gotten her acceptance letter to the school of her choice, the Rhode Island School of Design, abbreviated as RISD, which everyone pronounced "Rizdee." She'd gotten into their prestigious photography program, even though she'd neglected to inform them of her famous father's identity. I bet money they were going to be psyched when they eventually did find out, though. Tiffany's dad, Tassos, was one of the most sought-after fashion photographers in the world.

"Go, Tiff! Go, RISD! Go, Tiff! Go, RISD!"

"Portia's turn!" Tiffany called out, twirling Portia into the center of the circle.

"Go, Portia! Go, Sorbonne! Go, Portia! Go, Sorbonne!"

Portia went right into a series of moves that looked like something out of a stripper-pole exercise video. Everyone whooped and laughed, and I found I couldn't stop smiling. As much as I was going to miss my friends next year, their excitement and happiness were infectious now. Finally, all three of them got together to bump and grind in the middle of the circle, and Vienna climbed up on the first pew for a bird's-eye view of the action. While everyone else started hamming it up for the camera, Ivy grabbed my hand and pulled me toward the makeshift snack area—one of the choir pews where we'd set up a few bottles and a bunch of boxes of chocolates Vienna had stashed away for this exact purpose.

"What's up?" I asked Ivy, even as my stomach clenched. I knew exactly what was up.

"Okay, I know I said not to freak, but we have to talk about what happened back in your room," she said, pressing her fingers together to form a sort of steeple in front of her chest. "What the hell *was* that?"

"Technology glitch?" I surmised, laughing nervously.

"Right," she said with a dubious expression. "The lights in just your room go out, then both our cell phones ring at the same time with no one at the other end. How do you explain that?"

"Uh . . ." I racked my brain, trying to think of something that would sound reasonable. "Solar flare?"

She rolled her eyes. Behind us, Vienna and Lorna attempted to hoist Portia up on their shoulders.

"Reed, come on—"

"No, Ivy, *you* come on," I replied. For some reason I was finding it far easier to doubt the whole thing once someone else started to believe in it. "What are you trying to say, really? You don't really think something happened when we said the incantation. I mean, do you really think we're—"

"Really think you're what?" Astrid said, reaching past me to swipe a chocolate.

Ivy and I looked at each other, snagged. I stalled by grabbing a chocolate of my own and shoving it in my mouth. As I bit down, I almost gagged. Ugh. Hazelnut.

"We were just saying how lucky they are that they all got into their first choice," Ivy improvised.

"And I was just saying . . . do you really think we're not going to get in to ours?" I added quickly, toying with the locket around my neck. "Ivy's totally superstitious, so she thinks our chances are somehow, like, less now."

Astrid just looked at us, one cheek filled with chocolate, making her look part chipmunk.

"What do you think?" Ivy asked.

Astrid chewed slowly and swallowed. "I think you losers should stop worrying and start partying."

She grabbed both our hands and dragged us back toward the dancing, shoving us into the center of the circle, where we joined Portia—who was back on her feet—and Noelle and Tiffany. Noelle grabbed me up in her arms and, with an incredibly straight face, started to lead me in what I think was a cha-cha. Laughter bubbled up in my throat, and I vowed right then and there that I wouldn't think about Eliza Williams or the book of spells for the rest of the night.

Tonight was about my Billings sisters—the ones who were alive and well and by my side. Not the dead ones who were haunting my dreams.

JUST A DREAM

The lights on the dance floor throbbed to the beat of the music, which vibrated the floor beneath my feet. Every step was uncertain as I tried to weave my way through the crowd, shoving a bare-backed sumo-wrestler type with my elbow, taking the pinpoint stiletto of a black Louboutin in the toe. Everywhere I looked there were unfamiliar faces, all distorted by punk makeup and dyed hair.

Where was she? I knew she was here somewhere, but everyone was so tall, so sweaty, so . . . bizarre.

Suddenly, someone slipped past me, the silky smooth fabric of a black robe tickling the skin on my arm. I felt a cold whoosh in my lungs as the figure passed, and I turned for a better look, but whoever it was had already disappeared into the crowd. Then, out of the corner of my eye, another robe. My heart caught with fear. This person stood stock-still in the middle of all the mayhem, face completely covered by the heavy, black hood. But I could tell I was being stared at, so I quickly turned away . . . and slammed right into another hooded figure, its chest so solid I bounced off. I wanted to reach up and rip the hood free, find out who or what was underneath, but something told me not to. Something told me I wouldn't like what I found. Sweat popped up along my brow as I whirled off, fighting the crowd, desperate to get away. I tripped over someone's outstretched leg and suddenly found myself at the edge of the dance floor.

I took a shaky breath and laid my hand flat over my locket. Before me was the lobby of Billings House. There was the gleaming oak banister. The faded gold wallpaper. The framed photos of former Billings Girls lining the walls. The ancient but pristine Oriental carpet in the center of the floor. And there stood my friends. All of them. Wearing their black dresses, holding their candles. They smiled at me over the flickering lights. Noelle Lange, Kiran Hayes, Taylor Bell, Tiffany Goulborne, Natasha Crenshaw, Cheyenne Martin, Shelby Wordsworth, Vienna Clark, London Simmons, Rose Sakowitz, Portia Ahronian, Ariana Osgood. I looked down and saw that I was wearing a bleached white robe. My hair was combed out over my shoulders and gleamed in the candlelight. I felt warm and safe and at peace. Like those apparitions in their black garb could never hurt me. Then someone took my hand. I looked over and smiled.

"Astrid! There you are!" I said, throwing my arms around her neck.

"I've been here all along, love. Where have you been?" she asked. She smiled as I released her, and the girls began to chant.

"We welcome you to our circle. We welcome you to our circle. We welcome you to our circle."

I smiled at Astrid as she gazed back at me, her eyes full of pride. Then, out of nowhere, a black cloth bag descended over her face. Astrid let out a bloodcurdling scream as she was dragged backward, away from me and toward the door.

"Astrid!" I shouted.

I looked to the sisterhood for help, but they all simply stood there, their smiles placid, continuing their chant.

"We welcome you to our circle. We welcome you to our circle. We welcome you—"

"Help! Noelle! Do something!"

Astrid screamed and kicked and flailed. The door behind her opened and she reached out, clutching the sides of the doorway with both hands.

"Stop!" I shouted, moving toward her. "Leave her alone!"

For the first time, the person who'd grabbed her showed her face, appearing over Astrid's right shoulder. The straight blond hair. The condescending blue eyes. It was Cheyenne Martin.

"She's mine now, Reed," Cheyenne said through her teeth.

I whirled around to look at the sisters. The spot where Cheyenne had stood a moment before was empty. All that was left in her place was a pink cardigan sweater, in a pool on the floor.

"We welcome you to our circle. We welcome you to our circle. We welcome you to our circle," the sisters chanted.

Astrid let out one last, strangled scream as the door slammed behind her.

My eyes popped open. I was on my side on my bed. My room was

dark. My fingers clutched my pillow next to my face, and I was breathing hard. I closed my eyes for a moment, trying to press out the image
of Astrid's kidnapping, the eerie expressions of peace on the faces of
the former Billings Girls.

It was just a dream, I told myself. Just a dream.

Clearly it had been brought on by Noelle's recent "kidnapping."
And far too much chocolate at tonight's celebration.

I took a deep breath and rolled over onto my back. Already the
images were fading and my pulse was returning to normal. I moved
my foot and it hit something hard. My head shot up and I saw that the
book of spells was still open near the foot of my bed, where I'd left
it when I'd dozed off earlier. I thought about closing it and putting it
away, but my limbs were too heavy and tired to move. Instead I rolled
over onto my other side to face the wall.

Somewhere in the back of my consciousness I heard the soft, whispering sound of loose pages fluttering to the floor. Then my eyelids
drooped closed and I quickly slipped into a deep, dreamless sleep.

A SITUATION

At breakfast the next morning, Missy's table was surrounded by a bunch of girls in our year, everyone talking excitedly as they leaned in toward some kind of magazine or catalog. I tried to get a peek at whatever it was as I strolled by, but London saw me and moved her arm, blocking my view from the page. Still, I thought I glimpsed swatches of fabric, and I definitely saw Constance shove a huge color wheel into her bag.

A sinking feeling sucked at my stomach. Was it possible? Were they picking out paint and fabric colors for the new Billings House?

I placed my tray down across from Noelle's and she scowled, perturbed. "Since when does the reject table get to shoot *us* looks?" she asked, taking a sip of her coffee. "They've been looking down at me all morning."

"And you've just been taking it?" I asked.

Her nostrils flared slightly as she placed the mug down. "Let them have their fun. They think they've won a battle, but the war isn't over."

A thrill of anticipation shot through me. A couple of months ago Noelle had told me she had no interest in bringing Billings back. But now she sounded more than a little invested.

"Does this mean . . . ?"

Noelle smiled. "Oh, don't you worry, Reed. I've decided to make it my mission to crush Missy Thurber's every wish. If there's a Billings on campus next year, you'll be running it."

"But how?" I asked, thinking of Mrs. Lange and her promise that we could set things right. Had Noelle reconsidered exploring the book of spells?

"Well, remember the other day when I told you that Daddy would get you anything you wanted?" she asked, lifting her eyebrows over the tipped rim of her coffee cup.

I squirmed. Somehow I didn't like where this was going. "Yeah . . ."

"I think you should ask him to put in a bid for Billings!" Noelle announced. She placed her cup down with a clang. I gaped at her. She had to be joking.

"You want me to ask your dad to build me a million-dollar dorm so I can live in it my senior year," I said.

"Actually, it'll probably be more like ten mil." She lifted both shoulders casually. "And why not? You'll ask him when we go to the city this weekend for your birthday party. The timing really couldn't be more perfect."

"Noelle—"

"I have to say, Reed, I was a little annoyed at you for not having called him back yet, but now I realized you've been playing it all perfectly," she said, her eyes shining with pride. "Make him wait. Make him grovel. By the time we get there, he's going to be ready to give you *my* trust fund." She blinked. "Actually, don't make him wait *too* long."

"I really don't feel comfortable with this plan," I said tentatively.

"Do you want Billings back or not?" she asked.

"Yeah, but—"

"Then you should be willing to do whatever it takes to get it back," she said firmly. "That's the Lange way."

I swallowed hard. I didn't want to remind her right now that I wasn't a Lange. And Brennans weren't much for throwing money around. Instead, I decided to let the subject drop for now and reached for my orange juice glass.

"You *slept* with her?"

The entire cafeteria fell silent at the sound of Ivy's inhuman screech. I whirled around and saw her standing near the far wall of the cafeteria, under one of the larger paintings depicting a quaint street in Easton circa the turn of the century. The object of her rant was Gage Coolidge, one of my least favorite people at Easton, and Ivy's long-term on-again, off-again friend-with-benefits. He looked around nervously, his shoulders a bit hunched as he noticed the entire world was watching.

"Ivy, chill. It was nothing. And I told you, I was drunk."

"Like that's an excuse!?" Ivy shouted, her face red with rage. "You knew exactly what you were doing! Admit it!"

Gage reached for her. "Ivy. Baby. Stop it. You know I love you. I would never—"

"Don't say that!" Ivy cried, shoving him off of her. He hit the wall, and the painting over his head shimmied on its mount.

The Easton security team sprang into action. Two of the guards rousted themselves from their posts near the doors and started toward Ivy at a swift, but not panicked, pace.

"You're such a liar, Gage," Ivy seethed, her hands curled into fists at her sides. "You're a liar and a slut and a cheat! I don't know why I ever got back together with you!"

The painting tilted suddenly as one of its strings snapped. I gasped, but Ivy didn't seem to notice.

"Ivy," Gage implored.

"No! Just leave me alone, Gage! I hope you die."

Just then, the second string snapped and the heavy painting plummeted. Half the dining hall gasped; the other half screamed.

"Gage! Look out!" I shouted.

Everything happened so quickly it was all a blur. Gage looked up, his eyes widened, and he staggered sideways just in time to keep from getting his face flattened, but the corner of the frame slammed into his shoulder. His head hit a chair as he went down and landed, sprawled on the floor, the frame half covering his face.

"Oh my God," Ivy said, crouching next to him with her hands over her mouth. "Oh my God!"

"Miss, please. Step back." The security officers had swooped down at the last second. One of them took Ivy's arm and helped her to her feet. All around me people loud-whispered.

"Is he okay?"

"Could have broken his neck . . ."

"Why did it fall . . . ?"

I ran over to Ivy and put my hand on her back, just as Josh arrived from the other direction, looking scared and tired, with dark circles under his eyes. Ivy buried her face in my shoulder as the security guard carefully moved the frame. There was a gash across Gage's forehead and the blood had seeped onto the floor. I swallowed back a surge of bile.

"Is he okay?" Ivy whimpered, tears streaming down her face as she looked up at me.

I didn't answer. I wasn't sure. The second guard leaned in toward Gage's face, cocking his ear toward his lips.

"He's breathing," he said. "Call nine-one-one." The other guard did as he was told and the first guard stood up. "Nobody touch him. It's best if he's not moved."

"Oh my God, Reed, what did I do?" Ivy said quietly. "What did I—?"

"You didn't do anything. It was an accident," Josh said as I stroked her hair behind her ear.

"No, but . . . right before it happened, I imagined it happening," she whispered furtively. "I saw it. . . . I wished the painting would fall down on his head."

My blood stopped moving in my veins. I glanced at Josh and his eyes were wide. Ivy's words still hung in my ears as Gage suddenly awoke and looked around. "What happened?" He touched his fingers to his forehead, then swooned when he saw the blood.

"Don't move, son," the guard said, dropping to his knees next to Gage. "You had a blow to the head."

"See? He's fine," I told Ivy. "He's gonna be fine."

Before long, Gage sat up slowly with the help of the guards and was lifted into a chair. The entire dining hall breathed a sigh of relief, and there was a smattering of applause, like he was an injured football player who'd managed to limp off the field. Ivy took in a broken breath and nodded.

"Okay. Everything's okay," she said.

"Reed!"

We both jumped at the sound of my name. Rose and Kiki had just come in through the double doors. Kiki was dressed, but her hair was wet beneath her knit cap. Rose was still in her pink plaid flannel pajamas, her gray coat open and billowing around her.

"What's going on?" I asked.

"It's Astrid. She's . . . missing," Rose said breathlessly.

Instantly, every last detail of my dream from the night before flooded my brain, making me light-headed. Astrid. The black-robed figures. The lobby of Billings. The ritual. Cheyenne dragging Astrid away. I fell heavily into the nearest chair.

"What do you mean, missing?" Ivy said.

"I woke up this morning and she was gone," Rose said. "Her bed was a mess, which isn't unusual, so I figured she was in the bathroom, but she never came back. Her wallet's in the room and so are her art supplies, her iPod. She's just gone."

"Maybe she just went out for a morning walk," Ivy suggested. "Maybe she wanted some exercise."

"Astrid is allergic to exercise," Kiki said, holding herself tightly around her waist. "Something's wrong."

"Have you told anyone?" I heard myself say.

"The headmaster knows," Rose replied. "I just spent the last half hour in his office telling him over and over again that I didn't hear her leave." She pressed her fingertips to her temple. "Why am I such a deep sleeper?"

I glanced over at Noelle, who shot me a questioning look. Not so long ago, she and her grandmother had faked her kidnapping. Was it possible they were behind this, too, somehow? Noelle looked convincingly clueless, but she'd proven to be a good actress in the past. But why would she and her family want to mess with Astrid?

Or maybe *Astrid* was messing with *us*. She was the one who'd accused Noelle of scaring the bejesus out of us. Maybe she'd somehow found out that it had all been a joke and was getting back at us by pulling the same prank. It was definitely something she would do, with her wicked sense of humor. My panicked heart slowed slightly in relief at the thought, but then I remembered my dream. And I freaked out all over again.

At that moment the double doors opened with a bang, and in walked Headmaster Hathaway, trailed by four policemen in full uniform. Someone's walkie-talkie was bleeping and beeping and crackling, and once again the dining hall went silent. I looked over at Noelle again and she, like everyone else in the room, looked startled and sick. We'd been through this too many times.

"Attention, students!" Headmaster Hathaway shouted, stopping at the top of the center aisle. His skin looked gray under the glowing lights. The cops fanned out around him, standing in a line with their feet in wide stance, as if they were readying themselves to handle a stampede. The headmaster cleared his throat and lifted both hands. "No one panic, but we have a situation."

SELF-IMPORTANT

Headmaster Hathaway had imposed a curfew. Everyone was to be in their own dorms by 8 p.m. and in their own rooms by nine. The campus, meanwhile, was crawling with cops. Some in uniform, some in plain clothes, all with stern body language and serious "don't mess with me" glares. There was no chance we were going to be able to sneak off campus to the chapel without being stopped, or at the very least followed. So I sent out a text telling everyone in the BLS to meet me in my room at 7 p.m. No excuses allowed.

Of course, I didn't need to add that last warning. Everyone showed up, most of them early. We all wanted to be together, to reassure one another that everything was going to be all right. I had a bad feeling that what I was going to tell them wasn't going to reassure anyone.

I stood in front of my closed dorm room door. My friends were all gathered on my bed and on the floor. Everyone except for Kiki, who was pacing in circles near my closet like a caged animal, and Noelle, who had claimed my desk chair and was looking at me like she knew what was coming and was not happy about it. Oh well. Not even Noelle could have everything her way.

"You guys," I began, my heart fluttering with nerves. "There's something I have to tell you."

I looked Noelle in the eye. It was time for complete and total transparency. I'd kept so many secrets, had so many hidden agendas in the past two years. I was tired of lying.

"Noelle and I are sisters."

Noelle's eyebrows shot up. I guess she didn't think I was going to lead with that. But it was something that was going to come out sooner or later, and I felt like I had to tell them in order for the rest of the story to make sense.

"What?" Amberly blurted. She looked at Noelle as if personally betrayed. "Noelle? Is that true?"

"Yes," Noelle said, keeping her eyes trained on me. "Half sisters. It turns out my dad had a bit of trouble keeping it in his pants back in the day."

Vienna and Portia snickered, while everyone else seemed stunned silent. As distraught as I was, even I smiled. I should have known Noelle would find a way to make the telling of it less painful.

"So that's why your dad's paying for her party," Portia said.

"Great," Kiki snapped, pacing away from the corner. "What does it have to do with Astrid?"

I froze for a moment. I hadn't forgotten why we were really here, and I didn't want anyone else to think I had.

"I'm getting there," I said. "Just . . . hear me out."

And I told them everything. How Noelle and I had found the book of spells. How I'd said the incantation by myself that night and what had happened. How I'd dreamed about Eliza Williams and found the locket, and about the yearbook and how Eliza was definitely the girl in my dream. And then I told them that Ivy and I had said the incantation again, and what had happened directly afterward—that the lights had gone out and our cell phones had rung. Aside from some squirming and exchanged glances, my friends stayed mostly quiet.

"Now here's the part I'm really freaked out about," I said, my throat dry. "Last night I had another dream."

Kiki, who had stopped pacing as soon as I'd uttered the words "book of spells" and had been engrossed ever since, looked at me with an expression that was somehow both wary and intrigued. "About what?" she asked. "Was it about Astrid?"

I nodded. "Yeah. I dreamed that she was kidnapped."

"You did?" Ivy blurted, standing. "Why didn't you say anything?"

"Because I thought it was just a dream," I said.

"Well, who kidnapped her?" Kiki asked. "I mean, in the dream?"

I bit my lip, knowing this was not going to go over well, and fiddled with the locket. "Cheyenne."

There was a long, loaded silence as everyone in the room locked eyes with one another. And then they all burst out laughing. Everyone but Kiki and Ivy, who just looked sick to their stomachs, and Noelle, who shook her head, like, *What am I going to do with you?*

"Thanks for that, Reed," Tiffany said, getting up and patting my shoulder. "We all needed a good laugh."

"You guys, I know this sounds crazy!" I said as they all began to rouse themselves from their seats. "But first the locket is right where my dream led me and then Astrid goes missing right after I dreamed she was kidnapped? Isn't that a little—"

"Coincidental?" Rose said gently.

My mouth snapped shut as I realized I'd been arguing in *favor* of me being psychic. Or at the very least superintuitive. Which was exactly the opposite of what I wanted to be. I'd been hoping they'd tell me it was just a fluke, but now that they were, I felt somehow . . . betrayed. What was wrong with me?

"She's right, Reed. Please," Amberly said, shoving her arms into her coat. "This is a little self-important, even for you."

I felt that one like a shot to the heart. "What? I'm not trying to be self-important. I know it sounds crazy, but I need your help. I'm afraid to go to sleep. What if I have another dream? What if we're all in danger or what if—"

"Reed, come on," Noelle said. "I know we've had a lot of drama around here in the past, but this is Astrid. Personally, I think everyone's overreacting."

"What?" Kiki blurted, her eyes on fire.

Noelle shrugged. "Doesn't she have a history of doing stuff like this? Bailing from schools, freaking out her parents, trying to get attention?"

"It's true. She actually once called herself the Rebel Without a Clue," Lorna said with a laugh. There were a few amused twitters throughout the room, and I felt my shoulders slump.

"I wouldn't be surprised if she showed up here tomorrow morning with some souvenirs from Dollywood or something," Noelle continued.

"No. She would have told me if she was going anywhere," Kiki said, shaking her head as she clutched her arms at her sides. "Or she would have left a note for Rose."

"So because she didn't inform you guys, that means Reed's seeing the future in her dreams?" Tiffany said incredulously.

"And besides, weren't Astrid and Cheyenne, like, BFFs?" Portia said, pulling her hair out of the collar of her coat.

"Yeah, I mean, if Cheyenne was going to come back from the grave to kidnap anyone, it definitely wouldn't be Astrid," Vienna joked.

This time the laughter was louder and everyone started for the door.

"Unless Cheyenne missed her and just wanted to hang," Amberly added, preening as she earned an even bigger laugh.

I felt desperate as they started to file out into the hallway past me. I didn't know what I was hoping for anymore, but I loathed feeling like I was the butt of some joke when I was just trying to help.

"Hey guys, I almost forgot to tell you—I volunteered with the head-master to head up a group of students to put up flyers in town," Tiffany said, lifting her camera bag from the floor and settling the wide strap on her shoulder. "If you want to come with, we're meeting on the chapel steps tomorrow after fifth, and we'll get excused for the rest of the day."

"I'm in," Portia said.

"Me too," Rose added.

"You'll be there, right, Reed?"

There was something in Tiffany's question that sounded like an admonishment. Like she was taking me to task for wasting their time. Like she half expected me to say no, because helping find Astrid wasn't something a self-involved person like me would do.

"Yes," I said firmly, even though I wanted to shake her for not taking me seriously. For not caring enough to listen. For not trusting me. "I'll be there."

"Good," she said in a condescending tone.

She walked out and I wanted to slam the door behind her.

"If it's any consolation, Reed, I believe you," Ivy said.

I turned around. She, Kiki, and Noelle were the only ones left.

"I do too," Kiki said.

"You do?" I asked.

She lifted her shoulders and walked over to my desk, where the book of spells sat closed atop my laptop. Carefully she ran her fingertips over the embossed circle design. "There are a lot of things in the world no one can explain, and even more things no one ever talks about. I'm not about to claim witchcraft isn't real, just because I've never seen it for myself." She took a breath and hugged herself. "I actually think it'd be kind of cool to be a witch."

I gave her a small smile. I wasn't sure I was a witch, but at least she'd made me feel a little less crazy.

"Personally, I think you're nuts, but I love you anyway," Noelle said, picking up her Birkin as she headed for the door. "But I have to love you. You're my sister."

She smirked, lifted her hair over her shoulder, blew me a kiss, and walked out.

VIVID

I stared out the window that night, watching one of the newly hired security guards make his circuit of the pathway outside the dorms. As the day had gone on, the police presence had thinned, replaced by private security personnel brought in by the school. The gossip was that with no ransom note and no evidence of a struggle, the police were hesitant to categorize Astrid's disappearance as a kidnapping, or anything else sinister, until she'd been gone for more than thirty-six hours. As Astrid's best friend, Kiki had been interviewed for longer than any of the rest of us, and she'd come out of the headmaster's office red in the face and looking like she wanted to take a bite out of someone. Once we calmed her down, she told us that, just like Noelle had theorized, the police thought Astrid had simply split. Kiki told them that if Astrid had run off she would have taken her iPod, her favorite vintage Doc Martens, and her sketch pad, all of which were still in her room, but they'd simply told her not to go anywhere in case they wanted to talk to her again.

They'd called me in next, and I was so angry throughout the whole thing I spent the entire fifteen-minute conversation digging my fingernails into the underside of my chair. I told them I was positive Astrid hadn't left on her own, but when they'd asked me what made me so positive, I had stopped short of telling them about the dream. I wasn't *that* crazy.

Or maybe I was. Who knew?

The door to my room clicked open and my heart hit my throat. I whirled around to find Josh slipping through the door, looking relieved to have gotten there in one piece.

"Hey," he said. He crossed the room and wrapped his cold arms around me.

Talk about relief. I sank into him, placing my cheek against his shoulder. "Hey. Thanks for coming. There's no way I'm going to sleep alone tonight."

"This is one favor you can ask for anytime," he joked.

He rested his chin atop my head, and we both looked out the window again. The guard whistled as he strolled toward the front door of Pemberly. I couldn't hear the tune, but I could see his lips were pursed, a thin stream of steam issuing from them in bursts and starts.

"Did he give you any trouble?" I asked.

"Me? Nah. I move with the wind," Josh said with a smirk. He turned me around by my shoulders and gave me a long, soft kiss. "It's getting late. Should we do what I came here for?"

"Absolutely," I said.

I slipped into bed and he shed his shoes, coat, sweater, and jeans, tossing them all on my desk chair until he was wearing nothing but his white T-shirt and plaid boxers. I lifted the blankets and welcomed him in. He gave me another quick kiss and I turned around, cuddling back into his arms.

"Sweet dreams, Reed," Josh whispered, his breath warm on my hair. "Everything's going to be fine."

He curled his arms around me and I drew his hands up under my chin, clasping them inside mine. As my eyes fluttered closed, I almost believed he was right.

"Reed? What do you think of this?"

I looked up from the book of spells. Lorna stood in the center of Sweet Nothings, the Billings Girls' favorite boutique in Easton, with dozens of dresses slung over one arm, their hangers clinking together as she moved. Dangling from her hand was a gold chain, and on the end of the chain was a pendant. A locket.

My locket.

My hand darted to my neck and found it bare. My insides clenched with anger. Lorna had stolen my necklace.

"Reed?" she prompted. "Can you help me put it on?"

The tons of clothes were gone now. She held the chain open around her neck, waiting for me to clasp it. Swallowing my ire, I placed the book of spells aside on the bench on which I was sitting and stood up. Maybe it wasn't my necklace at all—just one that looked like mine. One step and I teetered on my heels. When I looked down, I was wearing a pair of vinyl, high-heeled boots. They didn't belong to me, but

I'd seen them somewhere before. For some reason, the sight of them made me tense, nervous, and sad all at once.

I took another step toward Lorna. She turned to face me, as if wondering what was taking me so long, when suddenly the necklace tightened around her throat. Lorna's eyes bulged and her lips pulled back.

"Reed!" she rasped.

"Lorna!" I took a step toward her. My ankle turned, and I grabbed a rack of sweaters for support.

"Reed! Reed, help me!" Lorna choked.

"She can't help you."

The voice sent a violent shudder down my spine as I tried to right my feet under me. Sabine DuLac glared at me over Lorna's shoulder, her hands clasping the two ends of the gold chain as she pulled. Her black hair was wild and unkempt around her shoulders, and her light brown skin looked waxy, almost gray. Her once-sharp cheekbones now appeared sunken and there were angry red circles around her green eyes. She was wearing a black robe with wide sleeves, the hood pushed back from her face. I tried to take another step, but the heel broke beneath me and I hit the floor. My hip exploded with pain. Sabine snickered as she looked down at me.

"Turnabout's fair play," she said.

I realized suddenly that my skirt had flipped up and my underwear was exposed to the world. Out of nowhere, dozens of faces hovered over me, laughing, and I remembered. These were Cheyenne's boots. The ones she'd used to embarrass Sabine last fall. I turned and looked up at the spectators—Gage Coolidge, Hunter Braden, Walt Whittaker, Marc Alberro, Sawyer and Graham Hathaway, Upton Giles, Thomas Pearson—and they were all laughing. I opened my mouth to scream at them, to get them to help Lorna, but nothing came out. And they seemed not to notice anything but my humiliation.

"She has no power here," Sabine said, her French accent thicker than ever. She turned her lips toward Lorna's ear. "She never had any power."

Lorna reached out to me with both hands, fingers stretched to their limit. Blood poured into the whites of her eyes. Her lips slowly turned blue. Sabine jerked her backward, cutting her neck with the chain. And then, finally, Lorna's head lolled sideways. She was dead.

"No!"

I slammed my forehead into the wall and woke up, seeing stars.

"Reed! Reed, what is it? What's wrong?

Josh pushed himself up on one hand. His chest heaved beneath the thin cotton of his shirt. I sat up, holding onto my head, biting back tears.

"It was Lorna . . . Sabine . . . Sabine choked her to death."

"What?" Josh drew me into his arms. I gasped for breath as I rested my cheek against his chest. I could hear his heart beating and it seemed to be racing even faster than mine. "It was just a dream," he said. "It's okay."

I closed my eyes and tried to believe him, but all I saw was Lorna's sagging head. Sabine's evil grin. Astrid being dragged through the

Billings door by Cheyenne. Rose's and Kiki's faces that morning when they'd come to tell me the news.

"Josh." I pulled away. "What if it wasn't just a dream? What if—?"

"Reed." He reached out and smoothed my hair with his palm. "Sabine is behind bars. She can't hurt anyone."

"Yes, and Cheyenne's dead, but Astrid's still missing," I replied.

I threw the covers off my legs and got up. I couldn't sit anymore. I had to think. I slid the locket back and forth on its chain, making a rhythmic zipping sound as I paced. "Reed, listen to what you're saying," Josh said, looking up at me. "What are you going to do, call the police and tell them you dreamed that Lorna was killed by a girl who's been locked up for two months?"

"Yes! No," I said, wringing my hands. "I don't know."

"Just take a deep breath," Josh said, rising. He put his hands on my shoulders. "The Astrid thing might still be a coincidence," he said. "This could just be a dream."

"Stop trying to calm me down!" I blurted, turning away from him.

I shoved my hair back from my head and pressed my eyes closed, trying to get those images of Sabine and Lorna out of my head. Trying to will them away. But they wouldn't go. If anything, the images only grew more vivid. They were stronger than most dreams. Starker. I could practically smell the new-clothing and leathery fresh scents of Sweet Nothings. Could practically feel those stupid boots pinching my feet.

"I know it sounds crazy, but it felt so real," I said quietly.

Josh blew out a sigh. "Okay, so . . . what do you want to do?"

I turned and looked at him, gratitude flowing through me. "You believe me?"

Josh's green eyes were full of pain and distress and concern. "I believe you're seriously upset, and I believe there's something weird going on around here. But then . . . when is there *not*?"

We both managed a halfhearted chuckle.

"Why don't you call Lorna?" Josh suggested. "Once you hear she's okay, you'll be able to sleep."

I glanced at the clock. It was after 2 a.m. But this was life or death. "Okay."

I grabbed my iPhone off my desk and hit Lorna's speed dial. As the phone began to ring, I closed my eyes and silently chanted.

Please pick up. Please pick up. Please pick up.

One ring. Two. Three. I looked at Josh, terror seeping slowly into my veins.

"Four rings," I told him.

He swallowed. "Well, it *is* the middle of the night."

Five rings. Six.

"Hello?"

"Lorna!" I blurted.

Josh's face flooded with relief. He put his hands over his eyes for a moment, then dragged them down to cover his mouth.

"Reed? What time is it? Did they find Astrid?" Lorna asked.

Instantly I felt beyond guilty. Not to mention stupid, gullible, and nuts. "No. I'm so sorry. I misdialed. Just . . . go back to sleep."

"Oh. Okay." Lorna let out a yawn. "'Night."

Then she hung up.

I blew out a breath and dropped the phone on my desk. "She's fine."

"Good," Josh said. "Are you okay?"

I nodded, chewing on the inside of my cheek. Already the images of the nightmare were starting to fade. "I'm sorry."

"It's okay," Josh said. He gave me a hug and kissed the top of my head. "I'm just glad I was here."

"Me too," I replied.

We dropped back into bed and Josh lay down, one arm around me as I rested my cheek on his chest. He held me tightly and I listened to his breath as it eased toward the steady rhythm of sleep. I turned my face toward Josh's ribs, my nose flattening against his side.

"Don't ever leave me," I whispered.

"I won't," Josh whispered back.

I smiled and closed my eyes. Seconds later he was snoring lightly. Seconds after that, so was I.

WAKE-UP BANG

I awoke from a solid, deep sleep to the sound of loud banging on my door. The pinkish purple light of dawn blanketed my room, and I was just blinking my blurry eyes at my digital clock when the door was flung open and Mrs. Shepard, our housemother, looked inside. Normally impeccably dressed, she wore a purple tracksuit and untied sneakers. Her brown hair was back in a ponytail, and there was a line of dried night cream along her jaw.

Josh and I sat up as one, clutching the blankets to our chests. Mrs. Shepard's mouth was open with an unspoken announcement, but she froze for a second at the sight of Josh. We were so frickin' expelled, it wasn't even funny.

Mrs. Shepard's mouth snapped shut. "Get up and get dressed. All students to the chapel in ten minutes."

Then she closed the door and was gone. It wasn't until that moment that I heard the commotion. Mrs. Shepard wasn't the only one banging on doors. There were some shouts, a few drawer slams in adjacent rooms, and the sounds of people whispering furtively.

"Oh God," I said, looking at Josh. The blankets were curled so tightly in my fists the seams were cutting my palms. "Oh God. Josh?"

His skin was waxy and pale, his curls sticking out haphazardly as he whipped the covers off and got up. "We don't know anything yet. Don't freak out. Maybe they found Astrid. Maybe it's fine."

I took a deep breath and nodded, but I felt as if no oxygen had made it past my nose. Josh quickly yanked his jeans on and reached for his sweater as I tried to make myself breathe. Tried not to think about Lorna. Tried not to imagine the worst.

We dressed quickly and raced across campus with all the other clumps of confused, bleary-eyed students. When we finally shuffled into the chapel, my eyes flicked to the pew where I usually sat with my friends, but no one was sitting where they were supposed to be. Guys were on the girls' side, freshmen were in the back, seniors along with juniors up front. Josh and I exchanged a glance and slipped into the end of the last pew. I looked around for Lorna and Constance, who was Lorna's roommate in Pemberly, but I didn't see them. Josh's arm had been locked around my shoulders from the moment we walked out the door of my room and it was still there. I leaned into him, noticing the expressions on the faces around me. Kids were scared, confused, tired, concerned. But it was the adults who really disturbed me. Housemothers and male dorm advisors stood along the walls of the chapel, men with their hair sticking up on one side, women devoid of makeup, none of them talking, none of them daring to look anyone in the eye. Their faces all held slight variations of the same emotion: dread.

"Any idea what this is all about?"

Noelle slid into the seat at the end of the aisle, forcing Josh and me to scoot toward the center. She'd taken the time to brush her hair and swipe on mascara and lip gloss. Apparently I'd gotten my sense of urgency from my mother's side.

I felt a sudden stab of righteous anger and turned to Noelle. "Tell me you and your grandmother had nothing to do with this," I said through clenched teeth,

"What?" Noelle said breathlessly.

"Tell me this isn't another test for me. Or for Astrid and Lorna. Just swear to me, Noelle."

A flash of irritation lit her eyes, but she blinked it away. "Reed. I swear," she said, laying a hand on my arm. "I have absolutely no idea what's going on."

I turned away, tears filling my eyes. I wanted to believe her, but at this point, I had no idea what to believe anymore.

"Wait . . . Lorna?" she asked. "Why did you—"

"This is about her," I heard myself say. "She's dead."

"What?" Noelle gasped.

"Reed, come on," Josh said, putting his hand over mine. "You don't know that."

He gave Noelle a look I couldn't read, and I closed my eyes as a tear slipped down my cheek. Just then, the double doors behind us closed quietly and I heard footsteps hurrying down the center aisle.

I didn't have to open my eyes to know it was Headmaster Hathaway and a troupe of police. The din in the room momentarily grew to a fevered pitch, then quieted to a lull, indicating that the headmaster had reached the podium. There was a slam, and I forced myself to look up. The headmaster, wearing a full suit but no tie, with a good growth of stubble on his usually razor-scoured chin, cleared his throat.

"Students and faculty, I'm afraid I have a grave announcement," he said.

Josh's arm tightened around me. I felt Noelle stiffen in her seat. Whispers whisked around the room.

"Despite our efforts to increase security, and despite the police presence on campus—"

I heard the sarcasm in his voice as he looked over at my old pal Detective Hauer, who stood in the corner in his usual uniform— rumpled blazer, creased shirt, cotton tie. *This is your fault,* the headmaster was saying silently. *I have to do this because you refused to take Astrid Chou's disappearance seriously.*

"Another student, Lorna Gross, has gone missing."

The collective gasp in the room was so predictable it was almost funny. But all I heard were the words *gone missing.* Not *been killed.* Not *died.* I felt an odd sensation that was somewhat akin to hope.

Meanwhile, both Josh and Noelle were staring at me. Josh because, I suppose, he was starting to believe that I was actually psychic. Noelle, I'm sure, wondering how I knew it was Lorna. I touched the locket around my neck and breathed in and out.

"The police have now launched a full investigation into both these disappearances," the headmaster continued, raising his voice to be heard over the whispered questions and quiet sobs. "In the meantime, the board of directors has decided that, for your safety, Easton Academy will close its doors until further notice."

Now the noise was uncontrollable. Several students stood up. Some even made for the door. There were shouts and slams and, somewhere, an out-of-place laugh.

The headmaster picked up a gavel and brought it down several times on the top of the podium.

"Silence! Silence, please!" he shouted. Everyone quieted immediately. "Just give me two more minutes of your time." His voice was uncharacteristically plaintive. Like he was begging for our patience, our sympathy, our help. He pressed both hands to the sides of the podium and bent at the waist, bringing his face close to its surface for a moment as he gathered himself. Double H was hanging on by a thread. For the first time since I'd known him, my heart went out to him. He took a deep breath and straightened up.

"Your parents and guardians have all been informed of the situation," he said, looking across the large, airy room. "Several students already have cars waiting for them on the circle, but please, before you leave campus, sign out with a member of the security personnel. There will be a guard stationed at the door of each dorm. I understand that the instinct is to flee, but we want to make sure each and every one of you is accounted for."

The students around me nodded, clutching hands, hanging on

his words as if he could somehow save them from whatever fate had befallen my friends.

"Before I let you go, I just want to say . . . we're going to do everything we can to locate your classmates and to ensure that Easton Academy's campus is secure going forward," he said. "In the meantime . . . please be safe." There was a long, suspended silence. The headmaster's eyes shone. "You are dismissed."

What followed was like a video I'd once seen of the running of the bulls in Pamplona, Spain. The guards at the doors barely had time to get them open before a burst of humanity spewed forth. Everyone was on his or her cell phone, frantically making travel arrangements or calling parents to see if arrangements had already been made. The sophomore guy who'd been sitting next to Josh vaulted over the back of the pew when he realized that Noelle, Josh, and I weren't moving.

"Reed. What happened?" Noelle asked slowly. "How did you know it was Lorna?"

"She had another dream," Josh answered.

"Lorna was . . . she was murdered," I said slowly. I looked up into Noelle's eyes. "By Sabine."

Noelle pressed her lips together and stared straight ahead. Sawyer walked by with his brother, Graham. He shot me a sympathetic look but didn't stop. Behind him were Rose and Kiki. They paused at the end of our pew, letting the other students filter out around them. Then Ivy was there. And Tiffany. Vienna and London appeared, clutching each other, which was interesting considering I was pretty sure they hadn't spoken in weeks. Portia and Amberly arrived together. Everyone looked grim as they gathered.

"Where's Constance?" I said.

"I saw the police bringing her into Hull Hall on my way over here," Ivy replied. "She was a wreck, but physically she looked okay."

"What the hell is going on?" Tiffany said, hugging herself as some of the faculty skirted by us. "First Astrid and now Lorna. This has something to do with us, doesn't it?"

I couldn't answer. How was I supposed to tell them about my dream? They'd all laughed at me just yesterday. And besides, even with all the evidence, I was having a hard time believing any of it myself. Because how could I suddenly be psychic? I wasn't even sure I *believed* in psychics. I touched the locket with the tips of my fingers and avoided eye contact.

"It looks that way," Noelle said. Her phone beeped and she took it out to check the screen.

"Reed, did you have another dream?" Kiki asked.

Noelle stood up and the other girls took a step back, as if she was radiating fire. "Let's not even go there," she said. "Right now we just need to concentrate on getting out of here and making sure everyone's safe."

Kiki glanced at me past Noelle's shoulder. "But what if—?"

"Reed," Noelle said, staring Kiki down. "Daddy's got a car waiting for us. Let's go."

I wasn't going to argue with that. I wanted out of there more than I'd ever wanted anything in my life. I looked shakily at Josh and he lifted a hand to my face. "Don't go home," he whispered. "If you can, go to New York with Noelle. I'll go crash at Lynn's apartment there. I'll be five blocks away."

I nodded wordlessly, tears slipping from my eyes. Then he kissed me and I got up and took Noelle's hand.

"We'll call you guys later," Noelle said, her voice slightly less forbidding than it had been a moment ago. "All of you just . . . go straight home."

The other Billings Girls parted to let us through, unwilling to mess with Noelle, and she hustled me toward the door like a girl dragging her little sister clear of danger.

ANCESTORS

"I know, Mom. I know. But I'll still see you on Friday for the party,"
I said as I threw my favorite sweaters and jeans into my duffel bag.
If there was a party, of course. I held the phone between my ear and
my shoulder, my neck straining as I flitted around my room, grabbing a lip gloss here, a notebook there, trying to figure out whether I'd
really need my history text and how long we'd be gone. "It would be
stupid for me to fly out there and then turn around and fly right back.
Hopefully by then Astrid and Lorna will be found and everything will
be okay."

"I just . . . I would feel a lot more comfortable if you were here," my
mother said. "With us."

I paused, a T-shirt balled up in my hand.

"I know," I said softly. "But being in New York . . ."

I'll be with Noelle. And, more important, with Josh, I thought.

"I'll be closer to school if it reopens and we have to come right back," I said. "And Mr. Lange . . ." I paused, swallowing hard as I recalled how intimately my mother once knew Mr. Lange—how intimately we were all connected. "I'm sure he'll have some serious security set up for us."

I shoved the T-shirt into my bag, then quickly added the framed photograph of me and my father—my real father—that sat atop my desk. Then I zipped up the duffel and tossed it toward the door.

"Okay. If that's what you really want to do," my mother said sadly. "Just call me when you get there. In fact, call me every hour."

I exhaled a laugh, my heart squeezing into a tight ball inside my chest. "All right. I will."

"Love you, Reed," she said.

My throat closed. I hadn't told my mother I loved her many times in my life. She'd spent most of my childhood on her back in bed, hopped up on prescription drugs and blaming my entire family for her sucky situation. Since she'd gotten sober last year, the words had been uttered between us more frequently, but now I was finding them harder than ever to say. Now that I knew she'd been lying to me about who my father was my entire life.

But then, I could be the next to go missing. If I didn't say it now, when would I have the chance again?

"Love you too, Mom. And Dad," I added quickly, clutching the phone so tightly it almost slipped out of my grasp like a greased pig.

"We'll see you at the big party," she said, trying to sound upbeat. "Be safe."

"I will."

I hung up the phone, shoved it in the back pocket of my jeans, and grabbed my pillow. Outside the open door of my room, girls rushed past with their backpacks and laundry bags, their teddy bears under their arms, their cell phones pinned to their ears. As I tossed my pillow toward my packed bag, I noticed the long, dingy laces of my favorite sneakers sticking out from under my bed and dropped to my knees to fish them out.

I pulled out the first shoe but had to flatten myself on the floor to dig for the other. As I grabbed it, my fingers grazed the edges of some folded papers. Grasping them between my thumb and forefinger, I tugged them out. As soon as I saw what they were, I sat back hard on my butt. The pages were thick and yellowed, frayed along one edge as if they'd been torn from a book. I unfolded them in my lap, and one hand fluttered to my mouth.

It was Eliza's handwriting, though slightly more haphazard and seemingly rushed than usual. From the size and the texture, I could tell that these were the pages that were missing from the BLS book. Suddenly I recalled the fluttering noise of falling papers the other night, when I'd woken from one of my nightmares. These must have been tucked somewhere inside the book of spells and tumbled out that night.

There was a commotion out in the hallway as someone dropped their suitcase and it burst open all over the floor. I got up shakily and closed the door, then sat down on my bed. Breathlessly, I began to read the pages.

I never would have believed the horrifying events of the past few days if I had not witnessed them with my own eyes, if my own heart had not been shattered by what has occurred. I realize the risk of putting these words to paper—of the danger myself and my friends might face if this book were ever to fall into the wrong hands—yet I must write them. I must record what has happened, if only to remind myself one day that I am not insane—if only to warn the coming generations of what has transpired.

I gulped in a breath. Eliza's terror poured off the pages. Pressing my lips together, I read on. Each line was like a fresh knife to my heart. Painstakingly, Eliza told the story of Caroline Westwick, a girl who had attended Billings a few years before Eliza had gone there, and about the coven Caroline's sister Lucille had started. She told of how Lucille wouldn't let Caroline in, and how Caroline had taken it personally, stolen the books, and cast spells on herself until she'd gone mad. She wrote that Caroline had committed suicide, throwing herself off the roof of the Easton chapel, and that her final words were "I don't belong."

Of course, we didn't know any of this when we happened upon the locket and the map that day in the garden. If we had, perhaps we would have been wary enough to stay away. Or perhaps not. We shall never know.

The next few paragraphs told of how Eliza, Theresa Billings, Catherine White, and Alice Ainsworth had formed a coven of eleven girls. Some of the girls were apparently reluctant but were convinced by Theresa's cunning. She described the night they had read the incantation, and what had happened just after the words were spoken.

A fierce, cold wind whipped through the temple, extinguishing each and every candle. We were all gripped with terror, but then, a moment later, only the candles we held in our hands flickered to life. Eleven points of light forming a circle in the darkness. We knew then that the spell had worked. We were witches.

My hand clutched my stomach. The light had gone out, and then their individual candles had flickered back to life. Just like that night in the chapel basement. Just like the night Ivy and I had said the incantation as well. My brain swam and I closed my eyes, holding back a wave of nausea. This couldn't be. It just couldn't be. Outside in the hallway a door slammed, and I opened my eyes, forcing myself to continue.

There were stories of fun spells—a boy with boils on his hands, a headmistress with a wayward skirt. Stories of celebrations with the coven, retellings that sounded so much like the gatherings I'd had with my own friends it was almost eerie. And then, just as I was feeling comfortable again, another part stopped me cold.

And then, a few nights ago, I had the dream. At the time, I thought it was nothing but a horrible nightmare born of my morbid imagination, but now I know it was so much more.

Eliza had dreamed that her friend Theresa and the maid, Helen Jennings, had thrown Catherine White into a ditch in the woods, killing her. And then, just a few nights later, Catherine died in almost that exact way. She was fighting with Theresa when Eliza happened upon them: A spell had gone wrong, and Catherine had fallen to her death.

I leaned back against my bed, trying to breathe. Catherine had *died*? All those times I'd read through the BLS book, I'd imagined the two of them together, hanging out on the Billings campus, reading books and flirting demurely with hot turn-of-the-century boys. But from the date on the entry, Catherine and Eliza had barely known each other a month when she'd died.

But this wasn't the worst realization of all. Eliza had a horrible nightmare that had sort of come true. Now I'd had two horrible nightmares that had sort of come true. Did this mean that Astrid had really been kidnapped? That Lorna was really . . . dead? My heart all but stopped inside my chest and I bent forward at the waist, fighting for breath as I was assaulted by the horrifying images from my dreams. This wasn't real. It couldn't be real.

I looked down at the pages in my hands and wished I had never found them. Whatever this was, I couldn't handle it. Whatever it was, I wished it was happening to anyone other than me.

After taking a few deep breaths, I forced myself to sit up straight again. Part of me didn't want to read any further, but I knew that I had to. I had to know. Stoically, silently, I read. I read about the coven bringing Catherine back to life. About how it had turned out to be some kind of monster and not Catherine at all. How the thing had attacked Eliza. How Helen and Theresa had saved her. How the thing had cursed all of them, and all of their ancestors, before finally falling over dead.

I felt sick and scared and confused. Did I really live in a world where things like this could happen? I felt like I was reading a horror novel, not a diary. But these things had actually happened to Eliza—or at least, she believed that they had. The sorrow as she described the night she and her friends had brought Catherine's body back to the site of her original death was so real. The description of how they'd buried the trunk full of books, and how Eliza had thrown the locket in the ditch as well, was detailed and vivid. As I read these last words, my hand touched the chain around my neck.

If Eliza had been so done with it, if she'd hated it enough to throw it away, why had she led me right back to it?

The second the thought crossed my mind, I scoffed at myself and got up off the floor. A thick fog cleared rapidly from my brain as I extricated myself from the fantasyland of Eliza's story and planted my feet firmly in the real world.

This was crazy. This whole thing was making me certifiable. A ghost hadn't led me anywhere. It was impossible. I was falling for all of this like some gullible moron, but it couldn't be true. No truer than Cheyenne sending me e-mails from the grave or leaving me spooky presents to find. All of that had had a reasonable explanation—Sabine had been trying to scare me. Clearly something similar was going on now. Someone was messing with me. It was the only explanation.

But how did they get inside your dreams, Reed? A little voice inside my head asked. *What about the dreams?*

Suddenly my door swung open and my heart hit my throat. Noelle looked me up and down.

"Get your coat on. Let's go."

"Wait," I said. I closed my eyes and held out the pages to her. "Please just read this. Just read it and tell me I'm not going crazy."

Noelle sighed with impatience but took the pages. As she began to read, all the color drained from her face. "Where did you get this?"

"It's Eliza's," I said. "It fell out of the book of spells. I'm pretty sure the pages were torn out of the BLS book at some point. Who knows when?"

I sat down shakily on my desk chair and Noelle sat on the edge of my bed. To my surprise, she slowly, carefully, read each and every word. The pages trembled in her fingers as she shuffled them.

"Somebody's messing with us," she said suddenly.

I took in a breath and waited for the relief to follow, but it didn't.

"What do you mean, us?" I asked.

"This," she said, standing and holding a couple of pages in each hand. "This doesn't just affect you anymore. It affects me, too." She put the pages back together and studied them. "Who could have done this? It's so freaking elaborate. I mean, look at the pages. They really do look ancient. Who could have known about—?"

"Noelle."

Her head popped up. She looked confused, like she'd forgotten where she was or that I was there too.

"What do you mean, it affects you, too?" I asked.

She hesitated a moment and I felt my blood start to boil. I'd told her everything. She'd better not even think about holding back from me.

"Girls!"

We both jumped as Mrs. Shepard stuck her head in the room. "Downstairs in five minutes!"

"Okay!" we both replied.

As soon as she was gone, I stood up to face Noelle. "What, Noelle? What is it?"

"Okay, *promise* you're not gonna read too much into this." Noelle took a deep breath. She folded the pages up, tucked them under her arm, and shook her hair back, lifting her chin as if ready for a fight. "Theresa Billings? She was my great-great-grandmother." She cleared her throat. "*Our* great-great-grandmother."

"What?" I blurted out.

My heart pretty much stopped. My eyes blurred as I stared at her, trying to figure out what this could mean.

"My father's mother's mother's mother," Noelle said, narrowing her eyes. "Yeah. I think that's right. Anyway, remember how annoyed I was when you found the BLS book in your room? That was because I saw her name on the list of members. I figured if anyone should have it, it should be me."

I nodded once.

"But now that I know we're sisters . . ."

"Yeah."

My brain would not go past one-word answers. It was like it was afraid to think beyond that. Everything beyond that was a swirling black void of horror.

"So that means that you and I are Theresa Billings's ancestors . . . ," Noelle said in a leading way.

Suddenly I felt like I was spinning and falling, spinning and falling, right down into the void. I clung to the back of my chair and tried to ground myself.

"So whatever that thing was that took over Catherine's body, when it cursed them, it cursed us," I said.

"Yeah. Sure," Noelle said with a scoff. "And I've got some crown jewels I'd like to sell you."

Suddenly everything snapped into focus. "Noelle, did you not read what Eliza wrote?"

"I read what *somebody* wrote," Noelle said with a dubious expression. "Clearly none of this is true, Reed. It's a piece of science fiction! This kind of stuff does *not* happen in the real world!"

"Fine. You think someone planted that in my room? Let's just see." My whole body shook as I walked over to my duffel bag, unzipped it, and yanked the BLS book out of the bottom, spewing clothes all over my floor. I dropped it on my desk with a bang and opened it right to the spot where the pages had been torn out. "Give me the pages," I demanded, holding out a hand.

Noelle rolled her eyes but handed them over. She stepped up behind my right shoulder and watched as I lined the torn side of the pages up with the torn scraps along the spine. My mouth went completely dry. The tears, the bumps, the shreds—all of them lined up perfectly.

"Nobody planted this, Noelle. Eliza Williams may have been crazy, but she wrote these pages," I said. "Whether or not any of this really happened, she believed that it happened."

Noelle glanced at me, her skin suddenly waxen. My experiment had clearly scared her. She took a step back, groaned, and covered her face with her hands.

"If you want to believe all of this, then you should probably have all the facts," she said. Her hands dropped, leaving behind momentary red fingerprints on her pale skin.

"What facts?"

"Well, there's something else," Noelle said. She looked at the pages and the book instead of at me, and tucked her hands into the pockets of her coat all casual. As if we were discussing the latest issue of *Vogue*. "And you're not gonna like it."

My heart hit my toes. Suddenly I realized the dorm had gone silent. Everyone had fled but us.

"What?" I said.

"Catherine White? This person who turned into some *thing* that cursed our family?" Noelle said, looking me in the eye. "She was a distant relative of Ariana's."

THE ARIANA CONNECTION

"Yes, Vienna, all bodyguards are welcome," Noelle said into her cell that night, rolling her eyes over her shoulder at me as she sat down on the chaise in front of her personal fireplace. "Okay. See you soon."

She ended the call and tossed the phone onto the settee next to her.

"That's everyone," she said, sitting back as if exhausted.

We'd just called all of the Billings Girls—including Missy, Constance, and London—most of whom were staying somewhere in the city, and asked them to come over. Ivy had been on her way to her home in Boston but had told her driver to turn the car around. Kiki, who lived in California, was staying at her aunt's place in Brooklyn, and Amberly's parents had put her up in a suite at the Waldorf with a pair of armed guards, and her mom was on her way out from Seattle via private jet to be with her.

"Missy was the hardest sell," Noelle said. "But she's coming."

"Good," I said flatly.

I dropped the magazine I'd been furling in my hand onto the bed and walked over to sit on the edge of the cushioned settee. Noelle's bedroom, on the second-from-the-top floor of her parents' opulent Upper East Side home, was roughly the square footage of the entire Billings House—or at least it seemed to be. Aside from the huge bedroom with its four-poster bed and massive fireplace, her suite had its own kitchen and bath, a living room, and a closet that could have fit both my bedroom and my brother's inside of it. Right now we were lounging in the cozy alcove adjacent to the foot of her bed, a real fire raging in the brick fireplace as snowflakes began to swirl outside the huge windows overlooking Central Park. With four guards placed throughout the house at her father's orders, I felt completely safe, and with the insane spread of food the cook had sent up for us upon arrival, I also felt cared for. Not that I had been able to eat a single bite.

"What are you going to say to them when they get here?" Noelle asked, crooking her arm behind her head and leaning back into it.

"I'm going to tell them what I found," I said. "One dream could have been a fluke. Two were a coincidence, but three?"

"So you really think you're psychic?" Noelle said doubtfully.

"I don't know, but I know that if I dream about your death next I'm going to warn you," I shot back.

We both turned to look at the fire. I watched the flames dance and thought of the flickering candles in Eliza's story.

"I have to ask you something," I said.

"I had a feeling," Noelle replied patiently.

"If you knew all along that Catherine White was related to Ariana . . . why didn't you tell me?"

Noelle blew out a sigh and sat up straight. She crossed her legs at the knee and placed her hands on either side of her on the delicate brocade of the chaise.

"Reed, it was ten million years ago," she said slowly. "I didn't think it mattered. To be honest with you, I'm still not sure that it does."

I let that one roll off my back. "But how do you even know?"

Noelle pressed her fingertips into the corners of her eyes for a moment, as if fending off a nasty headache. Then she stood up and walked closer to the fire, crossing her arms over her chest. She stared down into the flames for so long, I thought she'd forgotten I'd asked a question.

"At the end of our junior year, Ariana did a genealogy project for her sociology class," Noelle began. "She was always into that stuff and she took the project seriously—a lot more seriously than everyone else. While she was doing her research, she found out that her great-great-grandfather's sister, Catherine White, had gone to Billings at the turn of the century." She paused and looked up at the painting above the fireplace, a colorful, abstract rendition of the original Billings House that Noelle's father had commissioned for her a couple of years back. "I'll never forget how excited she was. She came running back to Billings like she'd just found out she was descended from royalty or something." Noelle looked at me over her shoulder. "She figured the relationship proved she was a legacy so she could get an invite to the Legacy the next year."

I narrowed my eyes, thinking back to all the invitation and plus-one drama last fall. "But she didn't."

"No. It turned out you had to be a direct line," Noelle said, sounding almost sad. "A great-great-great-aunt wouldn't cut it."

"Oh." I bit my lip. An ember jumped out of the fireplace and glowed on the slate hearth. Noelle lifted her foot and placed the toe of her boot on top of it, crushing the light out of it.

"So, if Eliza's story is true, then Ariana's great-great-great-aunt cursed our family for all eternity," I said.

Noelle turned around fully. "Weird, huh?"

"Actually, it makes sense out of a whole lot of crap," I replied.

Noelle arched her eyebrows. "So you think . . . what? Ariana murdered your boyfriend because she was playing out some kind of ancient curse?"

"I know, I know. It sounds insane. But isn't this all just a little *too* coincidental?" I said, touching Eliza's locket with my fingertips. "And don't forget Sabine. She was related to Catherine too."

Noelle shook her head, her expression irritatingly condescending. "Reed, Ariana killed Thomas because she was out of her mind with jealousy. And Sabine did what she did because she was plain out of her mind. Clearly there's something off in their DNA. It has nothing to do with a curse."

"Whatever," I said, standing. "What I want to know is, whatever happened to Eliza and her family? And what about Helen?"

"Google them," Noelle said lightly. "If we find out their kids all died in a fire or were born with two heads, then I'll believe you."

There was a rap on the door and Ginny, the head of security and the one female guard of the bunch, opened it. Apparently she was ex-Secret Service, and I could imagine she'd been very good at her job. With her broad shoulders, WNBA-worthy height, and serious scowl, she could intimidate anyone.

"Your guests are starting to arrive," she said, ushering Tiffany and Rose inside.

They walked toward us warily, and I saw Tiffany eyeing the food laid out on a buffet-style table near the far windows.

"Nice spread," she said, placing her camera bag down on the end of Noelle's bed. "Are we having a party?"

Rose, who looked tired and harried and scared, looked Noelle and me over slowly. "Why do I get the feeling you guys didn't invite us here to eat?"

I took a deep breath and looked at Noelle. She made a dismissive gesture with her hand, like, *This is your thing. You deal with it.*

"Let's wait until everyone gets here," I said. "I only want to tell this story once."

DISSENSION

"So this is why all this is happening?" Constance asked tremulously. "You guys are *cursed*?"

I had just read Eliza's entire entry to all of them, then explained the dream I'd had about Lorna. Ivy had squirmed up from her seat at my description of Eliza's coven's initiation, and I knew she was thinking the same thing I was—that Eliza's description of what happened after they'd read the incantation was exactly like what had happened to us. As the story went on, I saw Tiffany, Portia, and Vienna grow more restless and eye-rolly, while Rose, Constance, London, and Amberly looked completely terrified. Kiki seemed merely intrigued, her eyes never leaving mine as I spoke, but Missy simply stared straight ahead the entire time, her jaw set obstinately, as if wishing she could be somewhere else.

"We're not cursed!" Noelle said, throwing up her hands.

Amberly looked to be about five seconds away from being in dire need of smelling salts. She lifted her head weakly. "But Reed just said—"

"I know what she said, all right?" Noelle replied, pacing from the head of her bed to stand next to me in front of the gathering of our friends. "I just . . . don't think it's true."

"So what? You're good-cop, bad-copping us?" London asked, raising her eyebrows. She was wearing a high-neck, baggy sweatshirt and yoga pants, her dark, highlighted hair back in a ponytail. I'd never seen her look so demure in my life. "One of you tells us it's real, the other says it's all a joke? Are you trying to get us to, like, confess to something?"

"No," I said. "No one thinks that anyone in this room is responsible for anything."

"This is ridiculous," Tiffany said, standing. "I'm sorry, but I don't believe in witches and I don't believe in psychics and I kind of don't believe I stayed here this long."

"Tiff, please," I said, feeling desperate as she made for the door. "I don't know what to believe either. I just wanted to warn you guys, in case—"

"In case what? You dream about me next?" Tiffany said impatiently, whirling on me.

My mouth snapped shut and she took a breath, looking at me sympathetically.

"Look, I'm sorry. I'm just a little tense lately, okay?" she said. "I finally got into RISD, finally saw the finish line, and for once in our stupid high school careers everything was normal. All I wanted was some smooth sailing from now until graduation, and then *bam*. Astrid and Lorna go missing and here we all are again." She threw her hands up and twirled around once. "Back in life-or-death land," she said, widening her eyes sarcastically.

The other girls eyed one another, and it was clear that they felt the same way. "I know," I said. "It sucks. Believe me I know. But it's not my fault this is happening. I'm just trying to make some sense of it."

"Or maybe it *is* your fault," Missy said.

Everyone turned to look at her. Ivy clucked her tongue and rolled her eyes, turning away from Missy as if she were trying to keep herself from pouncing on her. Missy, who was sitting on a pillow with her back against the wall, leaned forward. "Missy," Noelle said in a warning tone.

"No. I'm totally serious." Missy shoved herself up from the floor, lifting her blond braid over her shoulder. "I believe you, Reed. It all makes perfect sense. You *are* cursed."

"What?" Portia said. "Girl, you are OOC."

"No, I'm not out of control," Missy said through her teeth, crossing her arms over her chest and taking a step forward. "Think about it. Everything was fine at Easton until *she* showed up. Then Ariana goes off the reservation, Thomas ends up murdered, Sabine comes to town and kills Cheyenne, then shoots Ivy," she said, nodding at Ivy's back. "Then you guys go away for break and Reed ends up kidnapped and left to die on a deserted island, and when you get back, *surprise*! Billings is leveled and now two of our friends have gone missing. You *are* cursed, Reed. We'd all be better off if you'd never come into our lives."

"All right. That's enough!"

I turned and gaped at Ivy. I think we were all surprised that the words had exploded from her mouth and not Noelle's. Missy turned red with shock but stopped ranting.

"Forget about everything that happened in the past," Kiki piped up, lifting herself up from the settee so that she was sitting on the arm, her boots resting on the expensive fabric of the seat. "Let's look at what's happening now. If Reed and Noelle are cursed, then why is it Lorna and Astrid who've gone missing? Where do they fit into all of this?"

Something passed through Missy's eyes at that moment. Some spark of knowledge. Some realization.

"What?" I blurted out, stepping toward her. "What do you know?"

The entire room went silent with tension. Everyone stared at us like we were two lions poised to attack.

"Nothing," she said, shifting her gaze.

"Bullshit," Ivy put in, storming over. "What the hell, Missy? If you know anything, you have to tell us."

Missy lifted her chin. "I don't have to tell you anything. You're the ones who decided I wasn't good enough to hang out with you anymore."

"Missy," Constance said, her voice tearful. "Please. Do you know something?"

"No!" Missy wailed. "No! God! I don't. Don't you think I would tell you if I did? Lorna's one of my best friends. Or she was, anyway," she added, shooting me another accusatory look.

"You know something. I can tell," Ivy said, grabbing Missy's arm. "Spill it, Missy."

"Get off me!" Missy cried, wrenching away from Ivy. She bent at the waist and grabbed her leather bag. "I should never have even come here."

Missy stormed past me toward the double doors, which were open to the hallway, Ginny and her partner, Goran, keeping watch just outside.

"Missy, wait," I begged.

"Forget it," she snapped, not looking back.

"Get back here," Ivy shouted, going after her. "Missy! You're not going anywhere until you tell us what you know!"

At that moment I swear I felt a burst of cold wind and both heavy doors slammed shut. Constance and Amberly screamed. Missy stopped in her tracks. If she'd been three steps further, those doors would have hit her. Slowly, I turned to look at Ivy. Her dark hair danced forward around her cheeks on a wisp of a breeze, before falling lazily down around her shoulders.

"What the hell was that?" Tiffany demanded.

"The wind," Noelle said, going over to an open window and slamming it closed. "I opened the windows because it was getting stuffy with the fire and everyone in here at once."

Shakily, Ivy turned to look at me. We both knew it wasn't the wind. It was just like that falling painting in the cafeteria yesterday morning.

"It's the incantation, isn't it?" Ivy said to me, as if no one else was there. "It actually worked."

Just then the two doors were flung open again, and everyone gasped. Noelle's grandmother, Lenora Lange, walked into the room, her high heels clicking against the marble floor. When she saw Ivy, she startled a bit, almost as if she could feel the fear coming off of her. Quickly, Mrs. Lange cleared her throat.

"Now, girls. We can't have this dissension," she said clearly, succinctly. She looked around the room, meeting each and every girl's eyes in turn. "If we're going to stop what's happening to your sisters, we're going to have to work together."

UNIQUE POWER

"The first thing you should know is that the curse is real," Mrs. Lange said.

My blood froze in my veins. No one moved—not Missy, not Ivy, not even Noelle. I felt as if there should have been an ominous rumble of thunder outside the window, but when I looked outside, all I saw were lazily swirling snowflakes and a dark blue New York City sky.

"At least, it's real to some people. Real enough for those people to be causing problems," Mrs. Lange continued. She walked over to the buffet table and poured herself a glass of sparkling water. She took a long sip before turning around again, cradling the crystal tumbler in both hands. The last time I'd seen Mrs. Lange she'd been all business in a suit. Today her short white hair was pushed back with a tortoiseshell headband, which made her sharp features seem softer. She wore a striped button-down shirt, a navy blue cashmere cardigan, and gray wool pants. But even in casual weekend wear, she commanded everyone's attention and respect.

"The Billings alumnae have long fallen into two categories," she said. "Those who believe in the curse, and those who do not. For the past fifty years or so, there hasn't been much evidence that the descendents of Eliza Williams, Theresa Billings, and Helen Jennings were actually cursed." She paused and gave a laugh. "Most of us have done quite well for ourselves. But those who believe happen to think that Reed has brought the curse to fruition by her presence at Easton."

My throat felt prickly and tight as I turned to face her. "What?" I said. "Why me?"

Mrs. Lange walked toward me, her eyes shining. She placed one hand on my wrist. Her fingers were cold and moist from the glass, but her grip was strong.

"Because, my dear, you are not just descended from Theresa Billings, but from Eliza Williams as well."

The room around me grew stiflingly hot, and everything blurred. Suddenly I saw Eliza's face in my dream. The curious way in which she'd looked me over. Her sad eyes so much like mine.

"The thing is," Josh had said in my ear as we stared at the annual, "she looks like you. A *lot* like you."

She'd had a foretelling dream, and now I'd had foretelling dreams. Her crazy, possibly psychic, possibly witchy blood was in my veins.

I took the water glass right out of Mrs. Lange's hands and chugged it, then choked on the bubbles.

"Reed," Noelle said, grabbing my arm. "Are you all right?"

I nodded as I coughed. The water fizzed up my nose and tears

stung my eyes. Noelle led me over to the cushioned bench at the end
of her bed. For a long moment I sat with my head between my knees. I
could feel my friends staring at me and wished they would all go away.
Wished that I would wake up from this nightmare like I'd woken up
from all the others.

Except I hadn't really woken up from any of them, since they were
all coming true.

"How?" Noelle said finally. "I don't understand how this is possible."

"Reed's mother's grandmother was Eliza's daughter, Catherine,
named after Eliza's old friend," Mrs. Lange said. "Catherine disowned
her daughter, Lea, when she decided to run off with a steel worker—
someone Catherine saw as beneath the family name. After that Eliza's
line fell out of wealth . . . but not out of spirit or strength," she said with
admiration in her voice. "That's evident in you, dear. This is why the
alumnae have taken such interest in you from the beginning: As both a
Billings and a Williams, you could have a unique amount of power."

I looked down at the locket, warm as always against my chest. It
had once belonged to Eliza. It had once belonged to my great-great-
grandmother.

"This is ridiculous," Missy said with a sneer. "She doesn't have
any power."

Suddenly I heard Sabine's words from my dream the night before.
She has no power here. She never had any power.

I stared up at Missy, my chest clenching. Was she was connected
to all this somehow?

Mrs. Lange turned to look at Ivy, who seemed startled by the attention. "You said the incantation, didn't you?"

Ivy looked timid for the briefest moment but then shook her hair back and lifted her chin. "Yes. We did. Just the two of us. How did you know?"

"I can see it in your eyes," Mrs. Lange said with a smile. "It worked. You two girls have summoned the power."

"No," I said, shaking my head, wishing this all away. "You need to have eleven girls for the incantation to work . . . right?"

Mrs. Lange sat down next to me and placed her hand on mine. "Don't you see, Reed? The fact that it worked just proves the theory. With both Theresa's and Eliza's blood in your veins, you can summon the power almost on your own."

A fizzing sensation began at the back of my skull and spread down over my shoulders all the way to my toes. Just like that, I knew. She was right. This was why I'd started having the dreams—dreams just like Eliza had. Because I had said the incantation that night in the chapel and summoned this . . . whatever it was. And Ivy . . . she'd moved objects without touching them.

Was this really all because of me? Because of who my great-great-grandmothers were?

"Ugh! I can't take this anymore," Missy spat. "I am *so sick* of hearing about the great Reed Brennan!" Her face was red and her eyes narrowed into angry slits as she glared at me. "You don't have unique power, Reed. Not magical or any other kind. Billings is going to be rebuilt without you, and you'll never set foot inside it again. And if you ever even set foot on the front walk, I'll be the first person to slam the door in your face."

She shot Mrs. Lange a withering glare and turned around. "If this insanity turns out to somehow be true, it doesn't mean you have double the power. All it means is you're doubly *cursed*!" she shouted back over her shoulder.

When she was gone, the only sound in the room was the crackling of the fire. Mrs. Lange took a deep breath and shook her head slightly, as if shaking off a small but irritating fly. Then she stood up and looked at the rest of the girls, all of whom were frozen, as in a tableau, around the fire.

"If any of the rest of you would like to leave, this is your chance," she said.

I stared at my friends—Noelle, Ivy, Constance, Kiki, Rose, Tiffany, Portia, Amberly, London, and Vienna—and wondered what they were thinking. Some of them looked scared, others annoyed, others sympathetic. But it was Constance's eyes that got me. She looked like she wanted to give me a hug.

I cleared my throat and stood, handing the empty glass to Noelle.

"Guys, I don't know if I'm psychic. I don't know if I'm cursed. And I definitely don't feel like I have some unique amount of power," I said, wiping my hands on my jeans. "All I care about . . . the whole reason why I asked you here . . . is keeping all of us safe. So please just . . . stay inside. Stay with your families. And if any of us calls anyone else, answer the phone."

"Even Missy?" Amberly said, her voice thick.

There was a halfhearted laugh. "Yeah. Even Missy," I said. "The best thing we can do right now is look out for each other."

"And if anyone's parents aren't around and you want to stay here, you can," Noelle added.

Slowly, everyone started to get up. They looked scared, but I could tell that they were glad they'd come. At least we knew we had one another's backs now. At least everyone had all the information. I hugged each of them as they made for the door, and Constance held on to me longer than anyone.

"Hey, Reed," Kiki said, pausing at the back of the group as the girls crowded through the doors.

"Yeah?" I said, suddenly exhausted.

"Call us if you have any more dreams," she said.

This time, no one laughed.

NEXT

"You're nothing, Reed! Nothing! You should never have been accepted at this school! You don't deserve to be here!"

My pulse thrummed in my ears as I backed across the Billings roof, Missy advancing on me with predatory ferocity in her eyes. Her black robe billowed in the wind, the hood jumping up and down on her back. As I tripped closer to the edge, my mind raced, trying to figure out a way out of this, praying that someone would glance up and see. I frantically looked toward Ketlar, willing Josh to run out the front door. Willing him to save me.

But something was wrong. Ketlar was not where it was supposed to be. I was looking at Billings from high above. I whirled around and realized that this was not the roof of my dorm at all. We were standing atop the Easton chapel.

How the hell had we gotten here?

"Everything was fine before you came here, Reed!" Missy continued ranting, her face practically purple with rage. "Thomas is dead because of you! Cheyenne is dead because of you! It's all your fault!"

"No," I said tearfully, even as the horrible guilt squeezed my heart. My head shook hysterically. "No. It wasn't me. I didn't do those things."

"You can't be that naive," Missy scoffed. "Those things were done because. Of. You!"

With each word, Missy shoved me toward the edge of the roof. Through blurry, stinging eyes, I searched behind her for the door—the door through which Noelle had tiptoed that night long ago, coming to rescue me from Ariana. The door was there, even though we weren't at Billings.

"You need to die," Missy said as the backs of my thighs hit the stone turrets along the side of the roof. "It's the only way. If you die, the curse will be broken."

My mind screamed at me to say something. To come up with the words that would convince her. But she was insane. She was out of her mind. Just like Ariana had been. Just like Sabine.

Then, behind her, the door opened and closed. My veins flooded with relief. But it wasn't Noelle coming toward us with a field hockey stick. It was Ariana. And her sadistic, murderous gaze was focused on the back of Missy's head.

"Missy!" I shouted. "Look out!"

She laughed. "Like I'm gonna fall for tha—"

Suddenly Ariana brought the hockey stick down across Missy's throat. Missy's eyes widened in surprise and terror.

"Ariana! No!" I screamed, buckling at the waist as tears poured from my eyes.

Missy's hands flew up to grip the stick, but her actions were futile. Ariana jerked the stick back and up with both hands. Missy started to scream, but her neck snapped and the sound died.

"No," I whimpered, as Missy went limp. "No, no, no, no, no . . ."

Ariana smiled placidly at me as she dragged Missy's body toward the stone wall and carelessly tossed her over the edge. A moment later I heard the thump of her body hitting the steps.

"Why," I sobbed, falling to my knees. "Why are you doing this, Ariana? Why?"

She turned and glared down at me, her eyes hungry like a rabid animal's. "You're next," she growled.

She pounced on me, her fingers curling around my shoulders as she let out a screech.

"No!"

I sat up in bed, gasping for breath, sweat pouring off my body. Noelle looked up from her pillow. "What is it? Reed? What's wrong?"

"Missy," I said with a gasp. "It was Missy."

At the same time, both our cell phones rang. I lunged for mine, saw Josh's smiling face on the screen, and picked up the call.

"Josh!"

"Reed! Are you all right?" he asked.

"What?" I blinked. "Yes, I'm fine. I just had another dream."

There was a pause. I could hear his ragged breathing clear as day. "I know."

A sinking feeling went through me as I realized what that meant. Then the bed shifted as Noelle got up. Eliza's torn pages fluttered to the floor and I realized with a start that Noelle must have been reading them in bed, after I'd fallen asleep. Slowly I turned to look at her, still holding my cell to my ear. She stood at the side of the bed, one hand holding back her thick hair, the other clutching her phone. Over in the fireplace, the last of the embers glowed red, throbbing like a heartbeat.

"Reed?" Josh said, sounding panicked. "Reed, are you there?"

"Okay. Yes, of course. We will," Noelle said grimly. "Thanks for calling me, Paige."

She lowered the phone. I'd never seen her look so scared. "It's Missy," she said to me. "She's gone."

THE CONNECTION

"I get it now," Noelle said, pressing her fist into her hand as she paced back and forth in front of the fireplace. "I see the connection."

Downstairs the house was full of commotion as Mr. Lange and his security team made phone calls, ordering up bigger and badder systems, probably tapping the phones or installing hidden security cameras or ordering up some vicious guard dogs. I sat on the bench at the end of the bed, my phone in my hands, waiting for it to ring again as it had been doing nonstop since the news had gotten out. Josh was on his way over, and I felt like I was sitting on a bed of pins and needles, waiting for him to walk through the door. Outside the huge windows the sun was just starting to make itself known, lighting the sky with pinkish-purple hues. It looked like it was going to be a beautiful day.

"What connection?" I asked Noelle, intimidated by her frenetic restlessness. "What are you talking about?"

"I know why they've taken Astrid, Lorna, and Missy," Noelle said, her eyes wide, as if she'd been mainlining espresso all night. She grabbed Eliza's pages from the floor, wrinkling the edges in her grasp. She flipped through them, reorganizing them, searching them frantically for something.

"Why *who* have taken them?" I asked standing.

Noelle groaned in frustration as her eyes scanned a page. "Look!" she said finally, holding one out to me. "Look what it says right there. Caroline Westwick's final words."

I didn't have to look at the page. I'd practically memorized it. "I don't belong."

"Right!" Noelle said. "Eliza says that Helen had a theory that everything went bad because a girl who hadn't been properly chosen and initiated had been let into the group."

"The coven," I corrected.

Noelle rolled her eyes, letting her arms and the other pages flop to her sides. "Fine, the coven. So if what Grandmother said about these alumnae factions is true, if there are really some crazy old bats out there who think that all this stuff is real, maybe they're trying to get rid of the people who weren't properly *chosen* to be in Billings."

A whoosh of realization nearly blew me off my feet. Astrid, Lorna, and Missy hadn't been vetted by the other Billings Girls and invited into the house like tradition dictated. They had been handpicked last fall by then-headmaster Cromwell when he'd been trying to do away with all the elitism he felt Billings House engendered.

"Noelle," I said, feeling a rush of excitement. "You're brilliant."

"I know," she replied, looking more like herself than şhe had since Paige's phone call.

Then the triumphant rush fizzled and died. Because if she was right, this wasn't over.

"That means Constance and Kiki are in danger too," I said.

"And technically Sabine," she added.

I narrowed my eyes. "Yeah. Can't say I'm that worried about her." I lifted my phone. "We should call them. And the police."

"The cops will never believe us," Noelle said, grabbing the phone from my hands. "We have to go tell Grandmother and Daddy."

I planted my feet as she tried to tug me toward the door. I'd only seen her father for five seconds upon our arrival. We'd basically exchanged hellos and that had been awkward enough. I had kind of hoped I could wait out the rest of my stay up here in the cocoon of Noelle's suite and not see him again until the big birthday bash, when there would be so many people present I might not actually have to talk to him.

"Reed? Come on," Noelle said.

I hesitated. She rolled her eyes. "You're going to have to be in the same room with him sometime."

"Fine," I said. "But you do the talking."

She smirked, took my hand, and pulled. "Just the way I like it."

FATHER AND DAUGHTER TIME

Mr. Lange sat on the edge of the leather couch in his office, his hands forming a steeple in front of his mouth as he listened to Noelle's story. Even though it was the crack of dawn, he wore expensive-looking gray trousers and a dark blue button-down shirt without a crease in sight. Not a hair on his head was out of place, but I supposed that wasn't difficult to manage with a close-cropped Caesar cut. His handsome brow was furrowed, and every now and then he'd look up at me furtively, as if checking to make sure I was still there.

This man slept with my mother. This man slept with my mother and made me.

I was in serious need of some air, but instead of hoofing it for the nearest window, I clutched Josh's hand. We sat together on the love seat in the U-shaped seating area. He'd arrived just before we walked into Mr. Lange's office, and I couldn't have been more glad to have him there. Part of me was dying to ask him about his dream—the one that had woken him up and inspired him to call me—but that would have to wait.

"If I'm right, Constance Talbot and Kiki Rosen are in danger too," Noelle said, glancing at her grandmother, who stood with her back to the window, wearing an impeccable royal purple suit. "We need to warn somebody."

Mr. Lange took a deep breath and blew it out. He leaned back, the couch cushions squeaking as his weight shifted. He didn't seem surprised by all this talk of covens and curses and factions.

"This is why I didn't fight when Hathaway told me he was tearing down Billings," he said gruffly. "This is why I want nothing to do with the new construction. Everyone who has ever been associated with that place is either off their rocker or dead."

Wow. So much for Noelle's idea about a new Billings being my birthday gift.

"Wallace."

"Sorry, Mother," he said automatically. "Except you."

She smirked and I almost laughed. It was kind of humorous, seeing a man of his size and stature scolded by his diminutive, elderly mom.

"Well, what do you think, Mother?" he asked finally.

"You don't believe me?" Noelle blurted out.

"Of course I believe you, Noelle," he semisnapped, his brown eyes annoyed. "But this is a serious situation. Would you mind if I asked for a second opinion?"

Noelle fell silent. Mrs. Lange took a few steps toward us, lacing her

fingers together, then unlacing, lacing, then unlacing. It was the closest thing to a nervous gesture I'd seen from her.

"I think you should make some calls," she said.

"Fine." Mr. Lange unfolded himself from the couch, rising to his
full six-foot-four height, his silhouette blocking out all the sunlight
from the window behind him. "Mother, if you'd call the Talbots and
the Rosens," he said, moving to the huge desk that stood in front
of the biggest wall of bookcases I'd ever seen. "I'm going to call my
assistant and have her cancel Reed's party."

Noelle and I exchanged a look.

"What? No." Noelle walked over and stood on the opposite side
of the desk, her fingertips grazing the surface. "Daddy, you can't do
that."

He held the desk phone's receiver in his hand but pressed his
fingertip into the connector button, silencing the dial tone.

"And why, exactly, can't I?" he asked, his gaze once again flicking
to me.

I cleared my throat and stood up, releasing Josh's hand.

"Because . . . if whoever is doing this is really after the Billings
Girls, they won't be able to stay away," I said.

"Which is exactly why we're canceling," he replied, speaking
slowly, as if I were somehow addled. My face burned and I looked to
Noelle for help.

"But Daddy, if we have the party, we hold the home-field advan-
tage," she said. "We can draw them in and pounce."

Someone in the corner cleared her throat. We all turned around to find Ginny, the head guard, raising a finger. "If I may say, sir, as a strategy . . . it's not bad."

"Using my daughters as bait is a good strategy?" he snapped.

My skin tingled uncomfortably. It was the first time he'd referred to me as his daughter. I reached back for Josh's hand, and he stood up and hugged me instead.

"I don't like it," he said unhelpfully.

"Sorry, Hollis, but I don't think you get a vote," Noelle said over her shoulder.

"Yes, he does," I said, my mouth half against his shirt.

He kissed the top of my head.

"Sir, I promise you that if you allow me to run the security for this event and to bring in the rest of my team, not only will no harm come to your family, but we'll catch whoever's doing this," Ginny said, her voice low with emotion. "Let me do my job."

Mr. Lange glanced at his mother. She gave the slightest of nods. He closed his eyes for a moment, pinching his forehead between his thumb and forefinger.

"Fine," he said finally. He dropped the phone back into its cradle. "But I want to see all security plans at least twenty-four hours before the party begins." Then he looked up at me and Noelle and wagged a finger between us. "And I'm not taking my eyes off the two of you the entire night."

"Sounds like a blast," Noelle said sarcastically.

Mr. Lange let out a sigh and looked down at his desk, shaking his head. "Is that it?" he asked finally. "Because I have a lot of calls to make."

"Come on, you two. Somewhere in this house there's some French toast with our names on it," Noelle said to me and Josh, heading past us for the door.

"Actually, Reed, I'd appreciate it if you'd stay for a moment," Mr. Lange said.

I looked up at Josh, gripping him even harder. "It's okay," he whispered. "I'll be right outside."

I nodded and let him go. Mrs. Lange and Ginny left the room as well, closing the door behind them.

"Have a seat," Mr. Lange said to me. He tapped the end of a pen atop his desk as he walked slowly around it. As I retook my place on the love seat, he sat down near the end of the couch again, kitty-corner from me. I pressed my legs together, clasped my hands atop them, and held my breath. He opened his mouth to speak, then shook his head and laughed.

"Wow. I normally don't have any trouble making speeches," he said.

"You don't have to make a speech," I blurted out. "I get it."

Although I got nothing.

"And I'm sorry I didn't call you back," I said. "I was just . . ."

I trailed off. What was I supposed to say? *I just wanted nothing to do with you?*

"It's fine. Don't worry about that," he said. He leaned forward with his forearms across his knees and pressed his fingertips together. "I'm sure you have a million questions. I just want you to know I have zero expectations here. As much as I'd like to get to know you, I can only imagine what you think of me, so I understand if you'd rather me just be the peripheral father of your best friend."

The humble nature of his words was so unexpected, I was touched. The few times I'd been in Mr. Lange's presence, he'd always been larger than life, in charge, and somewhat gruff. That he would soften so much for me had to mean something.

"Can I ask you a question?" I said.

"Yes. Anything." He leaned forward, forearms on his knees, and touched all ten fingertips together.

"How long have you known?" I asked.

His eyes grew wet almost instantly and he quickly looked away. "Since the day you were born," he said. He pinched his forehead again and blew out a sigh. "My mother, of all people, told me. I went to the hospital and saw you . . ." He got this faraway look in his eye. "You were so tiny. Tinier than Noelle had ever been." He paused for a fond, private laugh, then sighed once more. "I told your mother I would help her, that I would be involved in any way she wanted me to be. She thanked me and promptly told me to go away. She wanted your dad, to be your . . . well, your dad."

"And you were fine with that?" I blurted out, surprising even myself.

"No, actually, I wasn't," he said. "But it wasn't up to me."

"What about your wife? Does she know?" I asked.

There was a pained look in his eyes. "She does. I told her when I found out. We dealt with it." He took a deep breath and blew it out. "Can't say she was overly excited when you came into Noelle's life," he said, shooting me an apologetic look. "I can only imagine you noticed her somewhat . . . cool demeanor in St. Barths."

I nodded slowly. At the time I'd thought Noelle's mom was never around because she was flighty and eccentric, but she was just avoiding me.

"So until the day I was born you never knew my mom was pregnant with your . . ." I swallowed. "How did your mother know?"

He gave a rueful laugh. "That woman, like her mother before her, has always kept an almost obsessive eye on the old families—the Williamses, the Billingses, and whatnot," he said. "She probably somehow knew about you before your mother did."

I gave a small smile.

"Anyway, I just wanted you to know . . . I don't know . . . ," Mr. Lange said. "I suppose I just don't want you to be uncomfortable around me."

I looked him in the eye. "I'm not," I said, only realizing it was true as I said it. Suddenly I was glad he'd made me stay behind. "Thanks, Mr. Lange."

His eyes shone as he gave a tight, hopeful smile. "Anytime."

ALMOST FAMOUS

Everyone in the restaurant was staring at us. Not that I could blame them. It was a boring, cloudy Thursday afternoon, and with two huge bodyguards hovering at our table, their backs to the window, blocking the view of Park Avenue for the rest of the diners, we were conspicuous enough to draw interest. One girl at a nearby booth kept holding up her cell phone at odd angles, ostensibly trying to get a signal, when she was obviously trying to get a photo of Noelle. She probably figured she was famous and wanted to zap her pic off to Page Six. Noelle had clearly noticed and was playing her role perfectly, wearing her huge, dark sunglasses at the table, even though we were inside.

Sucker.

"Hey, guys," a female voice said.

Goran and Sam, our two escorts for the day, took a menacing step toward Ivy as she swung her bag to the floor next to the empty chair at our table.

"She's cool, guys," Noelle said, holding up a hand. They instantly backed off, like a pair of dogs on a leash.

"Hey, Ivy," I said with a weak smile.

It was good to see her, good to be out, good to at least be pretending that everything was normal. Or as normal as it could be, with a former NFL linebacker breathing down my neck, supposedly trying to make me feel safe. Of course, the man's neck *was* as thick as a tree trunk, so my guess was no one was about to mess with him.

"Sorry I'm late," Ivy said, scooting her chair closer to the table.

"You should be," Noelle said flatly. She touched each of her pieces of silverware, straightening them on the table. "You're the one who called this little meeting."

We both glared at her. Noelle lifted her shoulders. "What?"

I rolled my eyes and turned my attention to Ivy. "So? What's up?"

She waited for the waiter to lean past her shoulder and fill her water glass.

"Do you need a few minutes?" he asked, his tone clipped.

"Please," Ivy said politely, casting a glance at the closed menu atop her china plate. He gave a nod and hurried off.

"I've been thinking," Ivy said, placing her elbows on the table and clasping her hands. She leaned forward and lowered her voice to a whisper. "We should get the rest of the girls together and do the incantation before your party."

"Check, please!" Noelle said, raising a finger and starting up from her chair.

"Noelle!" I hissed as the waiter glanced over, confused, from a nearby table. "We haven't even ordered yet!"

Noelle lifted her sunglasses, pushing them back into her hair. Cell-phone girl finally snapped her picture, and Noelle shot her a look that could have knocked over a skyscraper.

"I'll hit the hot dog cart on the way home if it means avoiding this conversation," she said through her teeth.

"Just hear me out," Ivy said, raising her dark eyebrows. She pressed her lips together before adding, "Please?"

That must have been a tough word for her to utter to her worst enemy. Noelle seemed moved that Ivy had put in the effort. She rolled her eyes but sat down again, waving off the baffled waiter.

"Okay, fine. I'm always up for a laugh. Why in the name of Prada would I ever want to do this?" Noelle asked.

Ivy took a deep breath and blew it out. "When Reed and I said the incantation, something happened," she whispered.

"I know, I know. The lights went out and your cell phones rang," Noelle said, waving a hand. "Spooooky."

Ivy looked at me and I could tell she was starting to get agitated. I gave her what I hoped was a calming look.

"It wasn't just that," I told Noelle quietly, touching the locket. "It wasn't until after I said it in the basement that night that I started having the dreams about our friends. And Ivy . . ." I looked at her and hesitated. We hadn't talked about the things I'd seen her do, and I wasn't sure if she wanted to.

"I think . . . no, forget that . . . I *made* that painting fall on Gage's

head the other day," she said quietly. "And when Missy was walking
out yesterday . . . I saw the doors slam a few seconds before they actually did."

I knew it. I *knew* it.

"You're serious," Noelle said, her chin tucked. "You think you can
move things with your mind?"

Behind her, Goran shifted from one foot to the other, and he and
Sam exchanged a look. They were probably thinking they'd been hired
to protect a bunch of wack jobs.

"I know I can," Ivy said.

Noelle's eyes narrowed. "Okay, fine. Move this salt shaker."

She pushed a silver shaker toward Ivy across the linen tablecloth.
Ivy clucked her tongue. "It doesn't work like that. I have to be angry."

"Oh, really." There was a bang and Ivy's face turned red. She gritted her teeth and cursed under her breath, reaching toward her foot.
"Angry now?" Noelle asked, tilting her head with a smile.

"Did you just *stomp* on her *foot*?" I demanded.

"Just trying to help," Noelle said angelically.

"Ivy, I'm so sorry," I said, appalled.

"It's fine." She straightened up again and turned her chair toward
me, away from Noelle. "Look, I just think that if we're all going to go to
this party and act as bait, we may as well say the incantation first. If all
the girls can do stuff like we can do . . . maybe they'll be able to protect
themselves if anything happens."

I saw the logic of what she was saying. I just had zero confidence
that we could convince any of them to do it.

"Oh, please. That is so not why you want to do this," Noelle said, taking a sip of her water. "You just want it to be true. You want to be a real witch. Admit it, Ivy. You spent your entire childhood watching *Charmed* reruns on TNT and hero-worshipping Rose McGowan, didn't you?" Then she squinted and tilted her head. "Or no . . . you're more of a bitchy Shannen Doherty type. . . ."

Ivy gritted her teeth and looked me in the eye. "Is it okay if I kill her?"

I smirked. "I wouldn't try. Goran's packing." We both glanced warily at the bodyguard and the bulge on his right hip. He sniffed and shifted his jacket to try to camouflage it better. "Besides, without her we won't have eleven."

Ivy's eyes lit up. "Seriously? You'll do it?"

"Oh, come on," Noelle said impatiently. "You guys, just because some crazy faction of alums thinks this is real, that doesn't mean it is."

I shot her a silencing stare and whipped out my cell phone. "I'll start with Tiffany."

"I'll call Portia," Ivy said giddily.

Noelle rolled her eyes and summoned the waiter with a flick of her hand. "I'll have the salmon and they'll both have the heaviest pasta you've got on the menu."

"What?" I said, lifting the phone to my ear as it began to ring. "Why?"

Noelle crunched on a cube of ice and sighed. "Because maybe if I can lull you guys into a food coma, I can prevent this thing from happening."

BRIGHT SIDE

"Somehow I can't see Eliza and Catherine shopping for candles inside a Pottery Barn," I said as we stepped through the huge glass doors, out of the frigid cold and into the warm, airy shop on Fifth Avenue.

"Yeah, well, it's the one place you can always guarantee they'll have white candles," Noelle said, standing next to me. She sighed and shook her head. "I still can't believe we're doing this."

"Come on," Ivy said, breezing by with an empty wire shopping basket dangling from her arm. "They usually keep the candles in back."

Heaving another sigh, Noelle followed after Ivy and Goran trailed her, his head swiveling slowly from right to left as if it were on a timer. Noelle pulled out her iPhone to check her messages as she skirted a couple of little kids chasing each other with pillows. Sam and I tried to catch up, but a woman in a wheelchair cut me off and stopped in the middle of the aisle to inspect a mahogany desk. Glancing at Noelle's retreating back, I hooked a right and started to go around a table full of plates and napkins, when I spotted a silver clock on a shelf, shaped like an old-school airplane. The face of the clock was the front of the plane, and the hands were the propellers. My father would love it. And after my conversation with Noelle's dad the night before, I'd been feeling a lot of guilt about my dad, as if just talking to Mr. Lange were a betrayal.

I picked up the clock and checked the price. There was a red slash through the bar code on the sticker and the scrawled note *1/2 off!* Sweet. I always had a hard time finding gifts for my dad that weren't Pirates-, Penguins-, or Steelers-related.

Sam turned so that a middle-aged guy could get by us, and I felt suddenly uncomfortable. It was weird, being shadowed by someone I'd barely talked to.

"What do you think of this?" I asked, holding it up.

He frowned, surprised. "It's a plane clock."

I blinked. "Yeah . . . ?"

"Why would you want a clock made out of a plane?" he asked, his brow knitting.

"Because it's cute," I replied.

"Never understand what people will spend their money on around here," he said under his breath, shaking his head and looking off toward the door.

My face burned, but I chose to ignore him. Glancing around the side of the towering display, I saw Noelle and Ivy pause near the back of the store. I grabbed one of the boxed clocks off the highest shelf, then went to join my friends. Actually, I probably shouldn't have left those two alone for as long as I already had. Knowing them, they were probably fighting over whether we should get twelve-inch tapers or nine. A crowd of female shoppers in fur coats skirted right past me, one of them elbowing me aside as if I wasn't even there, and I bit my tongue. I stood on my toes to try to see over their shoulders as they walked toward the stairs to the second floor. I spotted the candle section, but Noelle and Ivy were suddenly nowhere in sight.

I paused near a basket of white votives and looked around. Where had they disappeared to?

Then, suddenly, my heart lurched. Had they actually disappeared?

But you didn't dream about Noelle and Ivy going missing, a little voice in my head told me.

Then I scoffed, unable to believe my inner voice thought *that* was a logical argument.

Sam had stopped at the end of the aisle, but he didn't seem perturbed that the others were gone. I supposed that as long as I was safe, he was doing his job. I scanned the store again, flipping my hair over my shoulder, trying to look casual. I didn't see Noelle's tall frame or Ivy's dark hair anywhere. All we were supposed to do was buy some candles. What were they doing? Browsing the linens section?

I tucked the plane under my arm and took off, walking the aisles at the back of the store one by one. Every time I came to a corner I told myself they'd be around the next one, but they never were. When I got to the kitchen section I paused to take a breath, and felt a sudden, foreboding tingle down the back of my spine.

Someone was watching me.

"Everything okay?" Sam asked,

I jumped and nearly knocked over a precarious stack of heavy white dinnerware.

"Yeah. I'm fine. I just . . . Where did they go?"

"Hang on," Sam said. He lifted his hand to his mouth and spoke into his wrist. "G? What's your twenty?"

He lowered his arms and waited. And waited some more. Then he took a few steps away from me and tried again. "G? Please respond."

Out of the corner of my eye I saw someone slip into the next aisle. Slim frame, long dark hair, dark skin. My heart leapt to my throat. I took a tentative step away from the wall and peeked between two shelves. The girl's back was to me, but I could see most of her profile. She wore her hair in a low ponytail, and colorful earrings dangled against her sharp cheekbones.

Sabine.

"Omigod," I said breathlessly.

Someone grabbed my wrist and I screamed, whirling around.

"God! Jumpy much?"

Paige Ryan stood before me, her auburn curls back in a plaid headband. I looked across the aisle again and came face-to-face with the girl I'd been ogling. She was Asian American, with dark brown eyes and a petite frame. She looked nothing like Sabine at all.

"Are you all right?" Sam asked, coming up behind me.

"I'm fine," I said through my teeth. "Did you find them?"

He nodded. "They're waiting for us at the front."

I let out a relieved sigh.

Paige looked me up and down. "What're you doing here?"

"Getting some air," I replied. "What are *you* doing here? I'd think that shopping would be the last thing on your mind, what with your cousin going missing."

"I needed a distraction," Paige shot back.

In her defense, she did look rather harried. She wore almost no makeup and had broken out across her forehead. Her gray cashmere sweater was pilly and she was actually sporting jeans, which I was certain I'd never seen her wear.

"Well, good seeing you," I lied, backing away.

"Hope you get to go back to school soon," she said through her nose, picking up a coffee mug to inspect it. "At this point you may have to do an extra semester."

"Thanks," I said sarcastically.

She took a step toward me, cocking her head. "And you won't be doing any of it in the new Billings. Not if I have anything to say about it."

Then she placed the cup back down on the glass shelf with a clang and strolled away. It was amazing, how much she sounded like Missy. Those two seemed to be a faction unto themselves. With a deep, cleansing breath, I turned around and headed toward the front of the store, my bodyguard in tow.

Noelle, Ivy, and Goran hovered near the door with their shopping bags. I gave them a quick wave as I joined the short line to buy my father his new clock. As the line inched forward I told myself to look on the bright side. Sure, there was a bodyguard tailing me, three of my friends were missing and possibly dead, and I'd just had a run-in with a bitch, but soon I'd have a Father's Day present for my dad three months early, and at least Sabine hadn't escaped from prison and started stalking me. Even on the worst of days, there was always a bright side.

NOELLE'S POWER

We sat in a circle in the middle of Noelle's private living room. The chairs and the couch were shoved up against the walls, and several gleaming silver trays of pastries and fruit were placed at the center of the cushy, dark pink rug. We'd kept the lights bright, and Noelle's current favorite playlist pumped through the speakers. Her theory was that if any of the girls realized why they were there before we told them, they'd bolt before we could ever get started. I saw no flaws in that logic.

"Okay," I said, sitting down between Noelle and Ivy, feeling nervous. We'd decided that making everyone wear full-on white was out of the question, but I'd donned my white roll-neck sweater and light jeans for good measure. I zipped the locket back and forth on its chain and looked around at my colorfully clad friends. "Let me tell you why we're here."

"You're gonna try to make us into witches, aren't you?" Vienna asked, her mouth full of chocolate éclair. She looked at me over her fingers as she licked them one by one. She was wearing yoga pants and a long-sleeved T-shirt that stretched across her stomach. Stress eating was starting to affect her usually fit body.

No one laughed or scoffed or moved. They all just gazed at me with varying expressions of expectation, annoyance, and fear. So much for them not knowing why they'd been invited.

"I'm not trying to make you into anything," I replied, glancing at Ivy. "We just . . . we figured that since there happen to be eleven of us—"

"Left." Kiki stared straight ahead, her hands pressed flat into the floor at her sides. Her earbuds hung around her neck and her hair looked limp and unwashed. "There are eleven of us *left*."

My heart was tight inside my chest. "Yes."

Suddenly the room felt very warm. No one breathed, it seemed, for an oddly long time.

"We thought it might be fun," Noelle piped up, turning a palm toward the ceiling.

"And *I* thought it might help us protect ourselves," Ivy put in.

"So you really believe all this," Tiffany said flatly, reaching for the fruit platter and dragging it toward her across the carpet. "You really believe that when you guys said this incantation, you developed some kind of power?"

I took a breath and shook my head. "I don't know what I believe, Tiff. I just know that if it *is* real . . . then Ivy's right. We might have a better shot of keeping ourselves safe."

"I can't believe you actually agreed to this, Noelle," Portia said with a nervous laugh.

"Yeah, well, I've already got a therapy appointment booked for tomorrow morning," Noelle joked. "Maybe Dr. Markowitz can help me sort out why."

The other girls laughed and I felt my shoulders relax a bit. Noelle didn't need any incantations. She was already so powerful. She had the ability to make everyone in the room feel chill, or turn them tense on a dime.

"Really, though, I just thought it might take our minds off things," Noelle said. "And besides, Reed would just *not* let it *go*," she joked again, rolling her eyes.

More laughter. I glanced at Ivy, who was clearly not amused, but I didn't care. If Noelle's tactic worked to get the others on board, I was all for it.

"So, what do you guys think?" I asked, glancing around.

Tiffany finished chewing her last bite of strawberry and closed her eyes. "I can't believe I'm saying this, but fine. I'll do it—if only to prove this whole thing is a joke."

"I'm in too," London said. She glanced at Vienna and blushed. "I think it'd be kind of cool to be a witch."

"Well, if she's in, I'm in," Vienna said, dusting powdered sugar off her fingers. She'd just downed another doughnut. "What do we need to do? There's no blood involved, right?"

"I'm not doing it if there's blood," Rose said, looking peakish.

"There's no blood involved," I assured them, feeling a rush of excitement so sudden and fierce it actually made me nauseous. I nodded to Ivy, who grabbed a small stack of papers behind her and started passing them out. "All we're going to do is hold candles and say this incantation."

Rose chewed on her lip as she read the words, kneading her hands together. Tiffany read it through once and put it aside, as if she'd already memorized it. Amberly's page shook as she held it, and a line appeared between her eyes as she concentrated. I held my breath, imagining that this was similar to how Eliza had felt when she realized her friends were going to join her. They were going for it. They were really going for it.

"This is never gonna work," Noelle whispered to me, leaning toward my ear.

I lifted one shoulder and bit back an unexpected grin. For the first time in my life, I was certain she was wrong.

ACCORDING TO PLAN

As I looked around the circle of my friends, candlelight casting their faces in dancing shadows, I suddenly felt like a complete idiot. Like the ringleader in some crazy endeavor to experiment with some new drug or base-jump off the Empire State Building or get everyone to shave their heads. This little undertaking was just as stupid, and potentially just as dangerous—at least as dangerous as the first two. Not that I would ever admit that out loud. Because I couldn't take another eye roll from Noelle without knocking her on the head.

Ivy returned to the circle after making sure everyone's candles were lit. She stood to my left, Noelle to my right. Directly across from me, Rose stared into her flame as if mesmerized and Amberly seemed to be blinking in slow motion. Kiki's jaw was set in determination, and Tiffany kept checking her watch. Portia toyed with her gold chains, her thumb hooked over the longest two as she ran it up and down the length of them. Vienna and London whispered, holding hands, and Constance just stared at me, like she'd follow me wherever I wanted to lead.

Somehow that scared me more than any of my nightmares had.

There was a round of deep laughter outside the closed doors of Noelle's living room, which exited onto the same hallway as the now infamous double doors to her bedroom. The laughter reminded me that time was of the essence here. It had taken a lot of convincing to get all the bodyguards and security personnel to leave us alone in here— Amberly's had pointed out that most threats came from "someone you know and think you can trust" (preaching to the choir, dude). I figured we had ten minutes tops before the whole army of them came banging down the door.

"Everybody ready?" I asked.

Nods and murmurs rippled around the circle.

"All right. Here we go."

"We come together to form this blessed circle, pure of heart, free of mind," I began. I was surprised by the strength of the voices around me, and it squelched my nerves a bit. "From this night on we are bonded, we are sisters."

I glanced at Constance, feeling a stab of guilt so intense it nearly knocked me over. Once upon a time I had sworn to be her sister, and London's too, and I knew how betrayed they'd felt when I'd formed the BLS and kept them out.

"We swear to honor this bond above all else. Blood to blood, ashes to ashes, sister to sister." I closed my eyes for the briefest moment, knowing what was coming. Or what was supposed to come. "We make this sacred vow."

I held my breath. A cold wind swirled through the room, and I heard a couple of people gasp. Amberly grasped Rose's hand and whimpered as all the candles flickered out. I glanced at Ivy, and she gave me a sly, triumphant smile. Then I looked at Noelle. Her face betrayed nothing.

The candles now extinguished, I waited. Then, slowly, they started to flicker to life again. First mine and Ivy's. Then Noelle's. Then Kiki's, London's, and Vienna's. Portia's glowed like a tiny pinprick, as if it were having trouble coming to life, but Rose's popped up so fast, she took a step back. Amberly stared at her candle, but nothing happened. I blinked, perplexed, and looked at Ivy. Tiffany's candle smoked for a second but didn't light. Constance's candle, however, was flickering merrily.

"That's weird," Ivy said.

"Nice trick, Reed. With the wind and everything," Tiffany said, looking around at the windows. Finding them closed, she cast her glance at the various air-conditioning ducts overhead. "How'd you time that one?"

"I didn't time anything," I said. "That's what happened when I said the incantation the first time. The wind, then the candle. At the time, I thought the wind had come down the stairs when Noelle opened the door, but . . . "

"There was no wind when we did it," Ivy said. "Just the cell phones."

"But my cell phone didn't ring," Amberly said, glancing toward her foot where she'd laid her phone on the floor.

"No. It wouldn't. Because we used the candles this time," I said, feeling impatient.

"So why didn't my candle light?" Amberly asked, her bottom lip puffed out petulantly.

"I don't know," I replied.

"And mine's barely doing anything," Portia said, waving it around like a Fourth of July sparkler. "WTF?"

"I don't know," I said again.

"So what does it mean?" Kiki asked, her gaze intense. "Are we witches or not?"

"Maybe *we're* witches and they're not," London said, waving a finger at Tiffany and Amberly. "Because, you know, our candles lit and theirs didn't."

"Or maybe the factory that makes the quote *magically relighting candles* unquote made a couple of defectives," Tiffany shot back.

"Tiff, we got the candles at Pottery Barn," Noelle said flatly. "As far as I know, they don't do trick candles."

"So what does that make me?" Portia said. "Some kind of weak-ass witch because my candle barely lit?"

"Maybe you guys just aren't believers," Kiki blurted out.

"You've got that right," Tiffany retorted.

Suddenly everyone was talking at once, throwing out theories, debating the reality of what they'd seen. I closed my eyes, the voices colliding and roiling inside of me, stretching my nerves to their breaking point.

And then, suddenly, a whistle split the air. I opened my eyes to find Noelle standing there with her thumb and index finger stuck inside her mouth.

"Everyone shut up!" she shouted.

They did, of course.

"Reed," she said, turning to me, holding her candle casually at her side. "This is your baby. What do you suggest we do now?"

I breathed in, counted to ten, then swallowed back my confusion, my excitement, my annoyance, and my fear—which was a mighty large pill to swallow. Everyone looked at me, hanging on my next words. I recalled Eliza's torn diary pages in my head and knew exactly what we should do.

"I think we should try out some of the basic spells."

NUTBARS

"This is one of the first spells Eliza and her friends tried," I said as we all gathered around the small round dining table near the bay window in Noelle's living room. It was a spot where she liked to eat croissants and sip black coffee while reading the Style section of the *New York Times* and looking out over the park, or nurse a hangover with the blinds drawn, depending on the day. Ivy, Kiki, Constance, London, and I leaned into the table, while the others crammed in behind us. Tiffany was over by the wall, scrolling through photos on her camera, the picture of indifference. I wondered if she was really uninterested, or if she was just posing as such. But if this spell worked, she would be convinced. All of them would.

If it worked.

"Well? What are you waiting for?" London demanded, pressing her hands onto the surface of the polished table.

I looked down at the ornate silver spoon we'd laid in the center of an old-fashioned doily. Was I really going to try to make the thing float? Suddenly I felt conspicuously unworthy, like the first time I'd played Grand Theft Auto with my brother's friends and kept driving my car into pylons while they cackled at me.

"Maybe Ivy should try it," I said, taking a step back. "We already know you can move things with your mind."

"Allegedly," Noelle snorted, fiddling with her hair.

"Fine. I'll try it," Ivy said curtly.

She stood so close to the table the edge made a dent in her plaid gabardine skirt. Her dark eyes squinted down at the spoon. I pressed my lips together and crossed my fingers at my sides.

"*Levitas,*" Ivy said.

The spoon jerked. Amberly screeched and covered her eyes. Someone else gasped. Tiffany shoved herself away from the wall, angling her chin up as if to see over Vienna's and Noelle's shoulders.

"What happened?" she asked.

"It moved," Amberly whimpered through her fingers. "The spoon moved."

"I thought it was supposed to float," Kiki said.

We all looked at Ivy. The spoon lay still, flat at the center of the doily. Her cheeks turned pink and she looked at the spoon again.

"*Levitas,*" she said, more firmly this time.

Again, the spoon jerked. It was now at an angle and clearly off center. Tiffany strolled over and peered down at it.

"Please. One of you is shaking the table," she said, rolling her eyes.

"I didn't," I said, raising my hands. I was standing a clear six inches away.

"Me neither," Kiki said.

Everyone turned to London, who was still grasping the tabletop. "What?"

Then she looked down at her fingers, clucked her tongue, and backed away, stuffing her hands under her arms. "It wasn't me, I swear."

"Try it again," Noelle ordered. Her hands were frozen, her fingers tangled near the ends of her hair.

Ivy sucked in an audible breath, clearly annoyed, and took a step back from the table. No one was touching it now. *"Levitas."*

Nothing happened. My heart sank so low I thought I might never be able to hoist it back up.

Tiffany laughed. "See?"

I realized for the first time that I had truly expected the spell to work, and my face stung as if I'd just come in from a jog in the summer sun.

"Why isn't it floating?" Ivy asked through her teeth.

"I don't know," I replied, touching my fingertips to my locket.

The group around the table started to break up and I could practically feel the skepticism radiating off of them. Not to mention their annoyance at me for wasting their time, and their irritation at themselves for having been sucked in. Honestly, I didn't blame them. I felt the same way. Except my feelings were directed at Eliza Williams and Mrs. Lange.

"Wait," Kiki said, grabbing the book of spells off one of the chairs where we'd left it. "Come on, you guys. Let's just try something else."

"I think we're done here," Portia said, lifting her black leather bag onto her shoulder.

"Guys, please don't go," I said. "I know you're upset, but let's try it again. Maybe we did something wrong. Maybe someone else should try it. It could be fun."

Amberly, who had more color in her face now that the experiment had failed, flipped her blond hair over her shoulder and tilted her head. "Since when is watching a spoon not move considered fun?"

A few of the girls laughed, hiding their smiles behind their hands. Suddenly everyone was walking toward the door. I could hardly believe they wanted to give up that quickly—but then I suddenly realized what it meant. It meant that they didn't actually *want* to believe. Not like Ivy, Kiki, and I did.

Maybe Kiki was right. Maybe that was why it wasn't working. What if all eleven members of the coven had to believe? If I took that theory and combined it with London's idea, it meant that Tiffany, Amberly, and Portia hadn't even believed enough to become witches during the incantation. And if the three of them weren't witches, that would weaken the coven, too.

"What are you thinking?" Ivy asked quietly.

I blinked, really listened to my thoughts for the first time, and felt ill. I was going off the deep end.

"Guys, just wait," I said loudly.

Thankfully, they all stopped. I grabbed for my messenger bag and pulled out a folder I'd stashed there before they'd arrived. I felt tired all of a sudden—beaten down.

"Just in case any of you is interested, I made copies of the basic spells page on Mr. Lange's copier," I said, handing them out. "Practice them at home. You never know. . . ."

Tiffany snatched the page from my hand, folded it, and stuffed it into the side pocket of her camera bag without glancing at it. She walked out without another word. London took one and looked it over, her expression serious. The rest came to me in a begrudging line, each of them taking her paper and tucking it safely away. I had no idea whether any of them would actually pull those pages out again, but how could they not? How could my friends not find this whole thing as intriguing as I did?

"Thanks, Reed," Kiki said, placing the book down and taking her homework page, as it were.

"Yeah, sorry it didn't work out like you wanted," Constance added, her paper fluttering slightly as she took it.

I looked at them both—the two who knew they were potentially in more danger than the rest of us—and swallowed back a warning that would probably only make them feel worse.

"Thanks for humoring me, you guys," I said.

They closed the doors behind them and about a minute later, I heard a loud group laugh as they waited for the elevator. Humiliation burned in my very bones. My friends were out there laughing at me.

"I don't get it," I said, turning to Noelle and Ivy.

"I know." Ivy flopped into one of the dining chairs, which we'd pushed off to the side, and slumped so low her hair hung down the back almost to the seat. "I swear I felt different after the first time we said the incantation. And I *know* I made that painting fall and those doors slam."

"Plus I didn't start having the dreams until after I'd said it," I added, leaning back against the table.

"Do you think there's something in what London said?" Ivy mused, folding her hands over her flat stomach. "Maybe it didn't work on Tiff and Amberly because they didn't believe in it, and maybe having two or three nonbelievers in the group weakened the incantation?"

I stood up straight. "I was just thinking the same thing!"

"You guys have completely gone off the reservation," Noelle said.

I flinched. I'd almost forgotten she was there.

"I don't believe any of this crap either, but my candle relit," she said, gesturing toward the pile of singed-wicked candles on a side table. "This is all one big ridiculous joke."

Ivy and I looked at one another, stunned and annoyed.

"But you said it yourself," Ivy countered, sitting up straight. "We got those candles at Pottery Barn, so how do you explain the fact that, like, eight and a half of them blew out, then relit?"

"I don't know, Ivy," Noelle said, throwing her hands up. "Maybe that gust of wind only squelched them for a second and then they came back. We've all seen that happen before. And maybe it hit Tiff's, Amberly's, and Portia's more directly and that's why theirs didn't relight."

"So how do you explain the wind?" I asked.

"This house is like a hundred years old," Noelle said, crossing her arms over her chest. "It's always been drafty."

Ivy and I rolled our eyes in unison.

"Whatever. I don't care if you guys agree with me," Noelle said. She grabbed the candles up in bunches and walked over to a thick metal garbage can near the door. "All I know is, your experiment didn't work. And there are still a bunch of nutbars out there who believe in this curse thing." She punctuated her points by throwing the candles into the can with a clang, one by one. "So if you don't mind, I'd like to focus our time and energy on finding out who those people are, and stopping them."

She slapped her hands together.

"Because when I find them," she said, "I am going to take absolute pleasure in personally kicking every one of their crazy little asses."

Then she turned around and flounced over to her bathroom, slamming the door behind her. A moment later we heard the bath running and the stereo flick on.

Ivy sighed and pushed herself up out of her chair. "Is it lame that I really thought it was going to work?" she asked.

My eyes darted to the offending spoon. "No," I said weakly, sadly. "I wanted it to work too."

BODIES EVERYWHERE

"Happy birthday, dear Reed! Happy birthday to you!"

I looked around the dining room at all my friends, my heart warm. I couldn't believe they'd all come out to Croton just for me, but there they were, gathered in my family's dining room, singing their hearts out with glee. My mother placed the birthday cake down in front of me, candles ablaze. I looked up at her before making my wish, knowing she'd be smiling back at me with pride. But then my heart stopped. It wasn't my mother at all, but a black-robed figure, its face hidden by a huge black hood. I gasped and looked around.

Noelle placed a paper noisemaker between her lips and blew. Sawyer Hathaway and Upton Giles exchanged party hats. Thomas Pearson laughed and slapped Dash McCafferty's shoulder as he doubled over. Over in the corner, Astrid, Lorna, Kiki, and Constance danced while London and Vienna checked out my huge pile of gifts. None of them seemed to see the dozens of black-robed figures dotted among them, stiff as corpses in all the merriment and chaos.

"Blow out your candles, Reed," a gravelly voice said in my ear.

I looked up at the creature who stood where my mother should have been. The heat from the candles blazed unbearably hot and my vision wavered. All the colors blurred around me. The balloons and streamers, the brightly hued dresses and crazily wrapped gifts—all of it faded together just as the voices and laughter swelled. This was too much. I was going to pass out.

Take a breath, Reed. Focus. They're here for a reason. They're going to hurt someone else.

I forced myself to stand and took a lurching step forward. Instantly I tripped over something solid and Thomas caught me by the arm.

"Watch out, new girl," he said, his blue eyes sparkling mischievously.

"Have a nice trip?" Gage put in, earning a round of laughter.

"Sorry, I—" I looked down and screamed. At my feet was a dead body. A girl, her face hidden beneath the bright paper tablecloth.

I turned around to run and tripped again. Another body. Another hidden face.

"No!" I screamed, clutching the first arm I could grab onto. "No!"

"What's your problem, Glass-Licker?" Ariana sneered down at me.

My heart clenched. I backed away from her and this time tripped backward, falling down hard. My hand came down on someone's torso. When I lifted it again, my fingers were coated in blood.

"No!" I screamed. "No! Someone help me!"

I reached up to my friends, but they didn't hear. Portia and Rose walked by me, stepping over dead limbs like they weren't there. Tiffany shouted something unintelligible and everyone laughed. My heart pounded frantically in my ears. Why couldn't anyone hear me? Why couldn't they see? The floor was covered with dead girls and all they could do was stand there and laugh?

"Help me! Somebody! Please, please, help me!"

Suddenly someone grabbed me by the shoulders and whirled me around. The person opened desiccated lips and screeched, *You don't belong!*"

I sat up in bed, screaming loudly enough to wake the dead. Noelle grabbed my hand just as Ginny, Goran, and Sam banged into the room, guns drawn. I cowered back toward the headboard and curled into a ball, attempting to catch my breath.

"What is it? What happened?" Ginny asked, holstering her weapon as she crossed to the bed. All I could do in response was whimper as the other two guards took off in opposite directions to check the other rooms.

"It was just a dream," Noelle answered for me. She ran a hand over my sweaty hair. "Reed? What happened? What did you dream about?"

I shook my head, squeezing my eyes closed in an attempt to blot out the images. But closing my eyes only made the memories more vivid.

"Was it Kiki? Constance?" Noelle pressed.

"No," I blurted, opening my eyes again. "It was . . . I don't know what happened. All I know was it was my birthday . . . and there were dead bodies everywhere."

Noelle's mouth set in a tight line. She looked at Ginny as she continued to stroke my hair.

"It's gonna be all right," Ginny said reassuringly. "We've got the party covered. Everything's going to be fine."

I nodded and let Noelle wrap her arms around me. Unfortunately, after everything that had happened, Ginny's words meant nothing to me. It had been a vivid, powerful nightmare. And lately, all my nightmares had been coming true.

PARTY, PARTY, PARTY

Since first arriving at Easton last year, I had attended some elaborate parties. Birthday celebrations on yachts, fund-raising parties at swank New York City locales, clambakes in Nantucket where the most basic thing on the menu was barbecued lobster meat in sweet-cream butter sauce. Not to mention the Legacy soirees—huge events with elaborate settings, attended by the most overly indulged, ridiculously privileged, stunningly beautiful kids on the Eastern Seaboard. But my seventeenth birthday party blew them all out of the water.

If I hadn't been so distracted trying to keep an eye on all my friends, I would've been having the time of my life.

The Lange mansion had three huge party-appropriate rooms on its ground level. First there was the grand foyer, with its marble floor, winding staircase, and two-story ceiling. Then there was the ballroom, which had literally hosted balls at some point in its history, and could therefore adequately hold upward of two hundred guests.

Finally, there was the dining room, which boasted fireplaces at both ends and normally held a gleaming oak table long enough to seat forty people comfortably.

Tonight that table had been removed and replaced by several cozy seating sections for people to lounge on while they noshed on seafood skewers and swigged five-hundred-dollar champagne. Colorful bubbles floated across the ceiling, and the sound of waves was being piped at a subtle level through dozens of hidden speakers. On the low tables at the center of each seating section were the aquarium centerpieces Noelle had promised, and along the walls stood elaborate arrangements of coral and sea anemones, which had somehow been animated to sway lazily, as if they were actually growing from the bottom of the ocean. The ballroom was set up for dancing, with colorful mesh eels dangling from the ceiling, undulating eerily and flashing different hues to the beat of the music the DJ was spinning from his booth. The walls had been papered with light blue and aqua green swaths of fabric, which heaved like waves, and actual sand dunes lined the walls.

I hadn't spent much time in there, however, because my friends had been keeping to the dining room, huddled together at two of the comfy seating areas. Whenever they did move, they were easy to track, since they stayed in a clump as they shuffled from room to room. Ironically, they reminded me of that old children's book, *Swimmy*, in which Swimmy the fish teaches his tiny friends to swim together in the shape of one big fish in order to keep the larger predators away. Just like the tiny fish, my friends were sticking together for safety.

I was glad they were taking the threat seriously, even if they hadn't believed in the book of spells. Unfortunately, Kiki hadn't arrived yet, and her absence was starting to make me tense. Especially considering she and Constance—who was currently downing a shrimp cocktail to my left—were the two under the greatest threat.

"You don't have to hover, you know," Noelle said, looking up at me as the latest group of well-wishers edged away into the crowd. "I can keep an eye on everyone."

"It's okay. I don't mind," I replied.

I glanced over my shoulder toward the corner where Goran and Sam were stationed. They had agreed to keep a reasonable distance so as not to cramp our style, but I always felt their eyes on me. Not to mention my mom's and dad's. At the moment they were standing a few feet away from the bodyguards, chatting with Constance's parents, whom they had just met. Luckily, Noelle's mom and dad were elsewhere. I'd yet to see my mother in the same room with my biological father, and I hoped I wouldn't have to—ever. Imagining how that scenario might play out made my head feel like it was going to explode.

Noelle got up onto her knees and leaned her hands on the back of the couch on which she, Portia, and Rose were sitting. "I didn't do all that planning just so you could stand there and not enjoy it. Go! Dance! Find your floppy-haired boy toy. I'm on babysitting duty."

I laughed and lifted one shoulder. I hadn't seen Josh yet tonight, and I couldn't wait for him to arrive. "Well, if you insist. . . . Thanks, Noelle."

She shooed me away and I finally turned, noting how Sam hopped into action the second I stirred. I greeted a few more guests as I moved through the door and into the foyer—some faces familiar, some completely new—and made my way into the ballroom. All the while my senses were on high alert, and I made sure to keep an eye out for anyone out of place, any strange movement, any prying eyes.

The music in the ballroom was so loud the floor shook beneath my silver shoes, and my rib cage seemed to radiate the beat. I paused for a moment to get my bearings in the relative darkness. I heard my brother, Scott, let out a whoop from somewhere near the center of the dance floor, and all I could do was hope he wasn't making too big of a jackass out of himself.

"Reed! There you are!"

Suddenly I was caught up in a quadruple hug. I recognized Kiran Hayes's signature flowery-musk scent before I ever got a look at her face. When I pulled back, there she was in all her supermodel glory. Just the sight of her brought back so many memories of my first days at Easton and Billings that my eyes flooded with tears. She wore a dark green dress with an elaborate ruffled collar that grazed her razor-sharp cheekbones and accentuated her olive complexion. With her was Taylor Bell, another of my first friends at Easton. Her curly blond hair was pulled back in a crazy ponytail and she wore an off-the-shoulder blue jumpsuit that made her look as slim as Kiran. The third set of arms belonged to Natasha Crenshaw, my former roommate and still good friend, whose royal blue dress was conservative but still accentuated her every curve. Her long black curls had been twisted into an elaborate bun at the nape of her neck, and her dark skin shone under the strobe lights.

"Guess Noelle gave you a heads-up on the color scheme," I said with a smirk, noting how their outfits complemented the décor.

"It's good to have friends in high places," Kiran demurred, taking a sip of her champagne. "You look amazing!"

"Thanks," I replied, looking down at my own dark aqua dress. The silk skirt floated around my knees like a cool breeze, and the portrait neckline played down my athletic shoulders. I'd found it at the foot of Noelle's bed that morning, inside a huge white box with a pink bow. The card read HAPPY BIRTHDAY—WALLACE LANGE. I had a feeling Noelle had actually picked it out, but I appreciated the gesture.

"Amazing, but tired," Natasha added, reaching for my hand. "Everything okay?"

I smiled, exhausted. Leave it to Natasha to not only notice my current state, but call me out on it.

"It's the birthday girl!"

Dash McCafferty burst from the crowd along with Gage and Trey Prescott, wrapping me up in a brief hug. His blond hair had been cropped short and he wore a suit so new it looked stiff. Still, he was one of the top five hottest boys in the room.

"It's good to see you, Dash," I said, a bit formally, giving him a pat on the back. I was still wary of any physical contact between the two of us after what had happened at last year's Legacy—and the aftermath.

"Hope you don't mind, P.A., but I didn't get you a gift," Gage said, swigging his scotch. "I've been laid up since the 'incident' last week."

He tried to do air quotes but dumped half his drink on the floor, splashing Taylor's shoes.

"Hey!" Taylor said, shoving him with one hand. "Watch it, Coolidge."

"Ooh! Look who's grown a spine since leaving Easton," Gage said, wagging his fingers at her. "Guess that's what happens when you matriculate at an inner-city PS."

"Well, you haven't changed," Taylor groused. She grabbed a napkin from a passing waiter and bent to swipe at her shoes.

As much as I wanted to catch up with my old friends, I needed to go check on the girls again. I was about to make an excuse to bail when someone grabbed my wrist. My heart hit my throat, but it was only Kiki, and my body flooded with relief.

"Reed. I need to talk to you," she said urgently.

"What's up? Is everything okay?" I asked.

"Yeah, I just . . ." She cast a furtive look at the others, but they were all debating whether Gage was a jerk or not. Like that was even debatable. "Some of it worked," she said, drawing me in closer.

My pulse thrummed in my ears. "Some of what worked?"

"The spells," she said through her teeth. "I've been practicing them, and I got a few of them to work."

Suddenly my mouth went dry. Someone whirled past, air-kissing me and wishing me many happy returns, but I didn't even register who it was.

"Are you kidding me?" I asked.

She shook her head slowly from side to side, not taking her eyes off mine. I tugged her away from my other friends toward the wall.

"Which ones?" I asked. I basically had the list memorized, though I hadn't tried any of them myself today. There had been too much to do in preparation for the party, but I was also kind of . . . angry at the book for failing me. I hadn't even looked in its direction since last night.

Yes, I was giving a book the cold shoulder.

"Well, *Levitas*, first of all," Kiki whispered, looking around furtively. "Forget the spoon. I made an entire set of silverware dance."

My pulse raced in my veins, tickling every inch of my body. "Seriously?"

"Yep," Kiki said, grinning. "And I got *Ventus* to work too."

I blinked. "Wait. You *made* wind?"

Kiki nodded proudly. "I moved the curtains in my room and everything."

I could hardly breathe I was so excited. "Kiki, do you realize what this means?"

"I know," she said.

I grabbed her hand and looked around. "Come on. You have to show me."

"Where? This place is crawling with people. Not to mention security detail," she said.

"I'll find a place."

We were just stepping away from the wall when a waiter stepped up next to us and handed me a small, square card.

"What's this?" I asked him.

"A message for the birthday girl," he said before moving on.

I looked at Kiki. That was weird. And weird, considering our current circumstances, was not good. I glanced behind me and felt bolstered by Sam's presence about ten feet away.

"Open it," Kiki said.

Fingers quaking, I tore open the small envelope. Inside was a flat card with a message scrawled across it in familiar handwriting.

> *Reed,*
> *Meet me in Noelle's room for a birthday surprise.*
> *Love,*
> *Josh*

I felt a momentary rush of relief, but it didn't last long. The last time I'd been passed a note during a party, it had been a fake—a note from Dash that had actually been from Sabine, telling me to meet him on the roof. And the rest was awful history.

Suddenly, my phone vibrated in my clutch. I exhaled loudly and yanked it out. It was a text from Josh.

STOP STRESSING. IT'S REALLY ME. I JUST WANT TO GIVE YOU YOUR PRESENT IN PRIVATE. NOW GET YOUR BUTT UP HERE!

I laughed, relieved for real now. I glanced at Kiki reluctantly. "I should go."

"That's cool," she said. "Just find me when you come back down."

"I will. Thanks." I shoved the note and the phone back into my bag and headed for the door. As much as I wanted to see Josh, my excitement was tinged with regret. If Kiki could really perform spells, I was dying to see it. Maybe I'd just have to cut the Josh-time short. I was halfway through the lobby when I almost collided with Noelle, Ivy, and the Billings pack.

"Hey! We were just coming to dance with the birthday girl," Noelle said.

"Actually, I'm on my way upstairs. Josh is up in our—your—room," I told her. "Distract Sam so I can slip away?"

"Are you sure that's a good idea?" Ivy asked, glancing up the stairs. "Maybe he should come with you."

"They're not letting anyone upstairs unless they're on the family's approved list," I said, gesturing toward the two beefy guards at the foot of the steps. "I'll be fine."

"Okay," Noelle said. "But come right back. I mean it. No naked birthday fun. Josh is just going to have to wait until the threat is neutralized."

I blushed hard and glanced at Ivy, who was also pink around the edges. "I have no intention of engaging in naked birthday fun," I assured them, wondering if Noelle had said that only to torture Ivy. "I promise, we will both return to the party in fifteen minutes. If we don't, you can call in the National Guard."

I turned around and started toward the stairs. Sam made a move to follow, but Noelle stepped in front of him, one hand to the center of his beefy chest.

"Let her go. She'll be fine," she said.

"But I—"

"It's her birthday and she wants some alone time with her man," Noelle told him. "So unless you want to be part of an illegal three-some . . ."

That was the last thing I heard before jogging up the steps. I laughed under my breath as I made my escape, my heart beating wildly, knowing that for once, only good surprises awaited.

HAPPY BIRTHDAY, INDEED

At the top of the carpeted steps, I turned left and made my way down the hall toward the elevator that would whisk me to Noelle's floor. It was amazing how muffled the sound was from up here. Aside from the dull thud of the bass coming through the floorboards from the ballroom and the occasional shriek of laughter, everything was silent. As I approached the small elevator alcove, my steps slowed. Usually light radiated out from the alcove at all hours, but right now it was dark.

I felt a cold wisp of a wind tickle the hair on the back of my neck, and suddenly, the gold locket felt warm against my chest. My hand fluttered up to touch it.

Images from my last dream flooded my brain. The birthday cake, the robed figures, the dead bodies. What was wrong with me? This had to be a trap. Of course it did. How could I have possibly thought it was a good idea to go anywhere alone right now?

I took an instinctive step back, heard a creak, and whipped around.

There was no one there. Down in the foyer, a glass shattered and was met by a resounding round of applause.

I should just go back to the party, I thought, taking one step in that direction. *Surrounded by a crowd, I'll be safe.*

But then, all I had to do was get in the elevator and it would take me right to Josh. No one could attack me if I was alone in an elevator. And I wanted to see him. Really, it was *all* I wanted right then. If I could just see him, everything would be fine. I turned around again and something caught my eye. A video camera bolted to the ceiling in the corner, trained right at me. I let out a breath, feeling foolish. Surely if someone shady had somehow slipped by the guards on the first floor—which was unlikely—and come up here, they would have been pounced by one of the dozens of security personnel. I was just being paranoid. Not that anyone could blame me, after everything that had happened to me in the past two years.

Steeling myself, I walked over to the alcove. The lightbulb in the overhead fixture was out. That was it. There was no sign that it had been tampered with—no shattered glass on the floor, no hanging corners or wires sticking out. No one was lying in wait. I hit the button and the elevator instantly pinged. My heart hit my throat.

Damn, I was jumpy.

The doors slid open and I stepped inside. As soon as I did I had this awful premonition that a hand was about to descend on my shoulder. I turned around quickly, but no one was there. Reaching out a violently shaking hand, I hit the button for Noelle's floor. The doors couldn't close fast enough. Every second it felt like someone was about to leap inside and grab me. Every moment a gloved hand was going to come around the corner and hold the door. By the time the doors finally did close, I was hyperventilating.

"Okay, calm down," I told myself, as the elevator ascended with an efficient hum. I leaned forward, resting my head against the cold, reflective gold doors. "Everything's fine. Everything's fine."

When the doors slid open again, I stepped out slowly, glancing left before I turned right. Again, I heard a creak. The door to the emergency stairs wasn't closed all the way. Had someone just come through there? Suddenly terrified, I sprinted into Noelle's room, slamming both the doors behind me, and whirled around, fully expecting to be jumped, blindfolded, dragged away. But when I turned, the only person standing in the candlelit room was Josh. He wore a blue suit and a dark gold tie. His hair was slightly neater and more styled than usual, and in his hand was a small red jewelry box.

"Hey, Reed." He pried the box open with a creak and a pop. Inside was a gorgeous square aquamarine stone, surrounded by tiny diamonds. A ring. "Happy birthday."

"What? What are you?" I tore my eyes away from the sparkling stone, which seemed to magically reflect every one of the dozen candles dotting the room, and looked at Josh. Suddenly I was breathless for a whole new reason. "Are you serious with that thing?"

Josh cracked up. He took a step forward. "Don't worry. It's not an engagement ring or anything," he said. He plucked the bauble from the box, holding the delicate gold ring between his thumb and forefinger. "It's your birthstone."

"I . . . I know," I said, stepping toward him. "It's beautiful."

Josh swallowed hard. He took my right hand delicately in his own and slipped the ring onto my ring finger. It fit perfectly and felt surprisingly light. "I just wanted you to know . . . how much you mean to me," he said earnestly, looking me in the eye. "If we were ten years older, I'd be asking you to marry me right now."

My heart expanded to fill my chest and tears stung my eyes, but this time they were perfectly happy tears. No fear, no anger, no nostalgia. Just happiness.

"And I'd be saying yes," I said.

Josh grinned. He pulled me to him and kissed me and kissed me and kissed me, until I seriously considered breaking Noelle's no-naked-birthday-fun rule. The room gradually seemed to grow warmer and warmer, until tiny beads of sweat broke out along the back of my neck, but we just kept kissing. His arms around mine, his chest to my chest, our knees knocking together. We kissed like it was the last time we'd ever have the chance.

"I love you so much, Reed," Josh said, finally breaking away. Our foreheads touched, and his hands were tangled up in my hair.

"I love you too," I said breathlessly.

It was a totally, utterly perfect moment. Then I heard a thud, and Josh's eyes went wide, and he crumpled to the floor. After that, all that there was in the world was my scream.

VILLAINS

"You are the strongest of us all, Reed. You're the only one who can save them. The only one who can save yourself."

Eliza Williams spoke directly in my ear. But I couldn't see her. Everything was dark. All I saw was blackness stretching out for all eternity. My head lolled to the side and I started awake, but even with my eyes open, all was black. My head radiated with pain.

"Use your power, Reed. Use it to warn them."

Frustration bubbled in my veins. I wanted to reach out and grab her. Shake her. Slap her as hard as I could. But I couldn't move my arms. How was I supposed to use my power to save myself? My power, if I even had one, was prescient dreams. And since I hadn't dreamed that someone was going to knock Josh out cold and grab me, the ship had basically sailed on using my powers for anything.

"Warn them, Reed. You can warn them."

I had no idea what she meant, and a whimper escaped my throat, waking me for another split second before I floated off into a new state of semisleep. I just wanted to know if Josh was okay. I just wanted him to be here, wherever here was. I scrunched my eyes closed as hard as I possibly could and thought of him. His eyes, his hands, his mouth, his touch. I wanted his arms around me. I wanted him to tell me everything was going to be okay. Forget saving myself right now. All I could think was, *I'm here, Josh. Please find me. Please help me.*

I saw him looking up into my eyes. Saw myself falling into him. His arms wrapping around me. Safe, safe, safe in his arms.

Suddenly the blindfold was ripped off my face, and a fingernail scratched my cheekbone. My head snapped back and slammed against something hard. I saw stars—brightly colored, flashing, popping stars—floating before my vision. I shook my head from side to side to clear it, and saw that I was in some kind of basement room. The ceilings were low, the floor was made of stained cement, and the only light came from several tall candelabras set up around the periphery. Tied to identical wooden posts, directly across from me, were Astrid, Lorna, Missy, and Constance.

Now I was fully awake.

"Astrid! Lorna! Missy! You're okay?" I blurted.

Tears streamed down Lorna's face, and Astrid was covered in what looked like dried mud. Neither of them looked anywhere close to okay. But they were alive. At least they were alive. But where was Josh? What had they done with Josh?

"Reed? What's going on?" Constance asked, her voice quaking.

She was still wearing her pink party dress, and a trickle of blood ran from her temple to her jaw. When had they taken her? How long had I been out? My fingers clenched into fists behind me, the simple movement straining my biceps. I looked down at myself for the first time. My ankles and my hands were lashed to a wooden pole. My shoes were gone and the skirt on my dress hung lower on one side, torn at the seam. Aside from the throbbing pain at the back of my skull, however, I appeared to be in one piece.

"I don't know," I said. "Just stay calm."

"Stay calm?" Missy shrieked. "What do you think those are for?"

She nodded toward the center of the circle and I forced myself to look. Laid out on a small round table were six pristine silver daggers, their points touching at the center of the circle, their black handles evenly spaced. Each handle pointed directly at one of us. It looked as if they had been set up to be grabbed easily.

Except there were only five of us. The sixth dagger pointed toward an empty wooden pole.

I felt a whoosh of movement behind me and turned my head, wincing at the pain. All I saw was a flap of black fabric, like a robe, and then it disappeared. My heart started to pound in earnest, thrumming white-hot terror through my veins.

Black robes. Just like in my dreams.

"Who's there? Who's doing this? Nice work nabbing five defense-less girls, you cowards. The least you could do is show yourselves!" I snarled.

There was a slam somewhere in the darkness, and Constance made a low, pathetic sound in the back of her throat.

"Good job. Now you've pissed them off," Missy snapped.

"Make that six girls," a disembodied voice growled.

A heavy door slid open, momentarily letting in a shaft of blue light. I saw that piles of crates lined the walls, stamped with the words ASTI MOVANTI over a drawing of some kind of quaint, rural village. Suddenly Kiki was thrown through the door, struggling and spitting and cursing loudly. A fresh red bruise rimmed her right eye, and blood dripped from a cut in her lip. Two robed figures had her by her arms, but they were barely holding on. The moment Kiki saw the rest of us, though, she stopped struggling. Her shoulders wilted in what looked like defeat.

"Run, Kiki," I said through my teeth. "You can still get away."

As far as I could see, she was our only hope. She was the only one of us who was semifree. But she just shot me a look I couldn't read and let them tie her to the post next to mine. I groaned and leaned my head back. We were screwed. We were ever so very screwed.

Taking a breath, I looked around, desperate for anything that could tell me where we were, anything I could use to get us out. I heard Eliza's words in my ear and clenched my teeth.

You can warn them. But who? It seemed like everyone worth warning was already here.

Still, I closed my eyes and thought as hard as I could of Noelle, of Ivy, of Josh. I conjured up a mental picture of the basement and tried to somehow make them see it. As if that were even possible. What really sucked was that it was the best—the only—plan I had.

"They're all here," a woman's voice said in the darkness. "We can begin the sacrifice."

My eyes popped open. Constance and Lorna whimpered.

"Sacrifice?" Astrid cried. "What sacrifice?"

"Anyone touches a hair on my head and you're dead," Missy spat, pulling against her ropes. "Do you have any idea who my father is?"

There was a chuckle in the dark. The sound was so out of place it sent a shiver down my spine. A hooded figure stepped from the shadows behind Constance and Missy and slipped sideways between them to enter the center of the circle. I sensed movement all around me, and soon we were completely surrounded by black hoods, outnumbered at least three to one. My eyes shot to Kiki and she looked back at me, her face grim, but somehow . . . determined.

Determined to do what? There was no way out of this. The only thing she should have been determining was whether she wanted to say any prayers before she died.

The figure in the center of the circle stood next to the table of daggers and ever so slowly turned, pausing as it faced each of us, as if it could see our faces through the dark fabric of her hood. It looked at Kiki, then Constance, then Missy, then Lorna, then Astrid, and then, as if moving through a thick fog, it turned to me.

It lifted its hands to its hood. I held my breath and forced myself not to look away. I thought of all my enemies. All the people who could possibly be insane enough to think up a horrible scheme like this. The figure looked slight, female. It was Paige Ryan. It had to be. Or Demetria Rosewell.

Just before the hood was nudged back, I had the panicked, wild thought that it was going to be Sabine. Or even Ariana. They had appeared in my dreams, after all. Could it possibly be one of them? Had they escaped?

And then the hood fell back and I gasped. I recognized the blond hair, the Botoxed brow, the perfect skin, the huge diamond earrings. It wasn't one of the villains from my dreams, but it was close enough.

It was Cheyenne Martin's mother.

MY EXECUTIONER

"Mrs. Kane?" I blurted.

So this was why I'd dreamed about Cheyenne. Her mother was behind this.

Cheyenne's mother smirked casually at me, as if I'd just told an inside joke. "Hello, Reed." She laced her skinny fingers together in front of her. "I've been looking forward to this moment for a long . . . long time."

I gaped back at her. Cheyenne's mother had never been anything but polite to me. She'd seemed so strong after Cheyenne's death. Emotional, sure, but strong. Not at all crazy. Certainly not a person who could mastermind the kidnappings of five of the wealthiest, most connected teenagers in the world—and me.

"Why?" I asked. "What did we ever do to you?"

Her smirk deepened. "Let's forget about 'we' for the moment, shall we? Let's talk about you."

Missy let out a wry laugh.

"Fine," I said, lifting my chin. "What did *I* ever do to you?"

From the corner of my eye, I saw Kiki's shoulders moving back and forth in an almost rhythmic pattern. I hoped she had come to her senses and was trying to get free. I decided to make this conversation last as long as humanly possible so that she'd have some extra time.

"I'm sure by now you know about our four founding mothers," Mrs. Kane said with a touch of sarcasm. "Of how Catherine White is related to Ariana Osgood, of how Noelle Lange is descended from Theresa Billings, of how you"—she paused here to sneer at me—"have both Billings and Williams blood corrupting your veins."

I felt a flash of pride and lifted my chin even higher.

"Well, I, too, am descended from that ignominious little club," she said, shaking a wisp of blond hair back from her face. "Cheyenne and I are direct descendants of Helen Jennings."

"The maid?" Kiki blurted.

Mrs. Kane's eyes narrowed and she slowly looked over her shoulder at Kiki. "Yes, Miss Rosen. The maid."

"What the hell is she on about?" Astrid asked Missy.

"Believe me," Missy said, "you don't want to know."

Mrs. Kane shot them a silencing glare. They both clamped their mouths shut.

"We always knew that if ever the four families were to meet at Easton again, there would be trouble," she continued. "But we had thought the Williams line had finally died out."

She stepped closer to me, her shoes rasping against the concrete floor. She leaned over and peered into my eyes, so close our noses almost touched.

"We should have known better. We should have known Eliza would rear her ugly head again. And so she has."

Her breath mingled with mine, and it was all I could do not to bite her nose off. She leaned back again and walked away, shooting me a snide look over her shoulder. "Your grandmother made sure of that, didn't she?"

Mrs. Kane plucked one of the knives from the circular table. My heart sank to my toes.

"What do you mean?" I said, barely able to speak past the burning lump of horror in my throat. "What do you mean, she made sure of that?"

Mrs. Kane cocked her head. "Don't you know?" She walked over and lifted the knife toward my face. I flinched, and Constance and Lorna started to sob. "You were engineered, my love." She brought the tip of the knife to my left cheek and I felt a pinprick on my skin.

"No no no no no," Lorna whimpered, wagging her head back and forth.

"Your grandmother was the one who invited your mother to interview at Lange Industries. She was the one who made certain your mother got the job as your father's assistant. She dropped in their laps the project that forced them to work late nights, weekends, holidays. To always be thrown together. She knew her son well enough to know what would happen. And as one of Eliza's descendants your mother is, of course, a whore."

"Shut up!" I spat.

She flinched and the point of the knife drove deeper into my skin. I felt the hot trickle of blood down my cheek and started to shake.

"Just like you are," Mrs. Kane continued, her voice singsong. She moved the knife to my other cheek and pricked me there as well. "All of the Williams women are whores, and all of the Lange women are manipulative liars. Guess what that makes you?"

She turned around and dropped the knife back on the table with a clang. "Clean it!"

Someone rushed forward and grabbed the knife, scurrying quickly away. Mrs. Kane turned back to me.

"Ever since you've been enrolled at Easton, there has been nothing but misfortune," she said, her words clipped now, as if she were giving a presentation on stocks and bonds. "My daughter died because of you and—"

"Your daughter died because Sabine DuLac was unhinged," Astrid spat.

Mrs. Kane blinked and her head twitched slightly. Then she continued as if Astrid hadn't spoken. "My daughter *died* because you are a walking curse," she said to me. "And the rest of you have only made it worse."

She flung an arm around at the others.

"Since you riffraff have been allowed into Billings, there has been nothing but misery and destruction. But now, with your sacrifice, the slate will be wiped clean."

The knife was returned to its place on the table, and Mrs. Kane's minion disappeared back into the shadows.

"With the purging of all those who were not properly chosen, all will be set right."

"You've got your facts wrong," I said. "I was properly chosen. And Missy would have gotten in. She's a legacy."

Mrs. Kane *tsk*ed, then sucked in a breath through her teeth. "You were chosen by one and one alone, Miss *Williams*," she spat. "Ariana Osgood, descendant of the one who cursed us, convinced the others to invite you in so that she could keep an eye on you. And then the little heathen went crazy and started murdering people. Hardly a ringing endorsement, I'd say."

"What about me?" Missy said, eyeing the knives with terror. "I would have gotten in junior year, like Reed said. You can't do this to me. It isn't fair."

Mrs. Kane ignored her. She lifted her hood back over her head and turned her back to me.

"Begin the ritual," she said.

And then she melted into the darkness. Instantly, six hooded figures moved into the circle. Each one picked up a knife. My heart slammed into my rib cage over and over and over again as I fixated on the point of the knife closest to me.

"No!" Astrid shouted. "You can't do this!"

"This isn't happening," Lorna said over and over again, still shaking her head. "This isn't happening, this isn't happening."

Missy continued shouting about being a legacy, and Constance was just screaming out of control. Her eyes were wild as she struggled against her ropes, and I felt as if my heart were slowly tearing with each shriek.

"Reed! Reed!" Kiki cried.

I somehow tore my eyes away from the knife, which was being walked slowly in my direction. The six wielders were muttering something under their breath—something like a chant—but I couldn't make out the words.

Kiki flicked her head back and I looked down at her hands. She was holding her left hand out, palm to the side, but her wrists were still bound. I looked back at her face, my brow knit.

"What?" I demanded.

She mouthed one word. "*Ventus.*"

She couldn't be serious. She wanted to try a spell? That was her master plan? Her eyes widened, prodding me. From the corner of my eye, I saw the person before me lift the dagger with both hands. I had about ten seconds to live. I nodded to Kiki, turned my hand so that the palm faced left as well, and shouted.

"*VENTUS!*"

Suddenly, a vicious wind whipped around the room, flinging my hair in front of my face, pelting my blood-soaked cheeks with dirt, stinging my eyes. I turned my head away from it to protect myself and heard knives clang to the floor. Someone screamed. Dimly I saw one of the robed figures crawling across the circle, grappling for a fallen knife. Then Mrs. Kane exploded from the shadows, her hood blown from her face, her hair flying wildly in all directions. She grabbed the figure's arms and pointed at me.

"Start with her! Start with the Williams girl!"

Shaking fingers closed around the knife handle. The robed figure stood up and staggered toward me, one hand holding the hood to her head. She lifted her arm and lunged. I closed my eyes, wondering how much this would hurt before I died.

Then there was a slam. The wind died. And someone who sounded a lot like my dad let out a guttural scream.

"No!"

A body careened against my executioner, knocking the figure sideways and slamming it into the floor. My father pinned the person to the ground, his knees on her shoulders, and wrested the knife out of her hands. When he whipped the hood away, my jaw dropped. It was Demetria Rosewell.

"Reed! Reed! Are you all right?"

Josh was in front of me. I began to shake from head to toe, with relief, with terror, with confusion. Had we really just done a spell? Or had the door opened at the exact moment we'd tried, bringing the wind with it? Was Josh really here, or was I dreaming again?

"Reed? Answer me," Josh said.

But he wasn't real. None of this was real. None of this could really be happening. In the corner I saw Noelle. And Ivy. And Mr. Lange. And Grandmother Lange. And about two dozen police officers. None of it registered, though. They were all characters in a play. Features in someone else's reality. I looked back down at my boyfriend, my eyes dry and narrowed, blood still dripping onto my shoulders.

"Reed?" Josh reached up and touched my face with his fingertips. His skin was warm. His fingers trembled. "Reed, please?"

He was real.

"Josh?" I blurted. "Josh?"

"Oh my God, you're bleeding," he said.

Someone started messing with my hands. Tugging at the ropes.

"Josh?"

I couldn't stop saying his name. Something inside of me had broken, and I was like a skipping record.

"Josh? Josh? Josh?"

His face changed. The color drained and his eyes were like pinpricks.

"Get her down," he growled.

Something slipped from my ankles and my feet were free. A second later my hands were too. I fell into Josh, launched into him, nearly flattened him. I was shaking so hard my head bumped his chin over and over and over again.

"Josh. Josh. Josh. Josh. Josh."

"It's okay," he whispered into my hair, kissing my head, holding me as tightly as he could. "It's okay. I found you. I found you and everything's going to be okay."

The weird thing was, it was almost exactly how I had imagined it a few minutes earlier. Exactly how I'd wished it to be.

SHARED BLOOD

"Drink this."

I sat on a chair someone had found in a corner of the basement, a coarse NYPD-issue blanket over my shoulders. Josh crouched in front of me, holding out a paper cup full of water.

"I'm an idiot," I said.

Josh blew out a sigh. "Well. I'm glad to hear you say anything other than my name, but I can't agree with that."

I swallowed hard. My mouth was full of dust and dirt and blood. I lifted the cup to my lips, shaking so hard some of the water spilled over onto my lap. I sipped just a little, and a trickle of clean coolness slithered down my throat. I stared down at the ring he'd given me. A spot of blood had dried over several of the diamonds.

"How can you love me?" I asked, my voice cracking. "All I do is bring you misery and . . . and head wounds. How can you even be with me?"

A single tear slid down my cheek and got caught in the crusted blood, where it stopped and started to itch. Josh laughed quietly. He lifted his hand to cup my cheek, drawing his finger over the spot, driving the itch away.

"How could I *not* be with you?" he asked.

I sniffled. "But I—"

"Reed, none of this is your fault," he said. "I know you don't believe that right now, but I'm going to spend the rest of my life doing everything I can to convince you. You're not cursed. You're not unlucky. You're perfect."

He hugged me and I leaned into him, pressing my nose into his chest. Over his shoulder, I could see the police rounding up the suspects—the believers. I was surprised that Paige Ryan wasn't among them, and happy to see that I didn't recognize anyone else, except dimly from the society pages. I had feared that Susan Llewelyn, once one of my favorite alums, would be part of this, but thankfully, she wasn't there either.

"Can I ask you something?" Josh asked, whispering in my ear.

I nodded into his jacket.

"Did you try to . . . send me a message?" he asked.

I drew back, my heart thumping extra hard. "What do you mean? Why?"

Josh swallowed hard, looking freaked. "I was with the police and Mr. Lange, Ivy, and Noelle, and all of a sudden I got this . . . I don't know . . . this picture in my mind. Of a crate of Asti Movanti."

We both looked toward the door, where dozens of Movanti crates were stacked.

"You . . . you did?" I asked.

He nodded. "I just sort of blurted it out and Mr. Lange said it was the name of this wine . . . some failed venture of Mrs. Cox's. She bought controlling stock in this Italian company or something and the wine turned out to be swill. I don't know. But anyway, as soon as I said it, Ivy told them we had to check out the Coxes' house. Because they live right next door to the Langes, and Mrs. Cox . . . she's a Billings alum and—"

He paused and took a breath. "That's her," he said quietly. "Over there. With the white hair."

I glanced up to find a frail-looking woman with a short white coif being inched away in handcuffs.

"Did you lead me here?" he asked.

"You are the strongest of us all, Reed. You're the only one who can save them." Eliza's words sent a shiver right through me. *"Use your power to warn them."*

Was it possible? Had I actually sent Josh a telepathic message? Had I saved us all?

"Where is she?"

I straightened up at the sound of my mother's voice, forgetting everything instantly.

"Mom!" I shouted.

Her face went slack when she saw me, and she raced over. Josh helped me stand up and I hugged her, clutching her to me as hard as I could.

"Are you all right?" she asked, leaning back and holding my face with both hands. "My God, what did they do to you?"

"I'm okay, Mom," I said. "I'm fine."

Behind her, near the door, I saw Grandmother Lange watching us. She had a proud gleam in her eye that made me want to hurl something at her. Was what Mrs. Kane had said about her true? Had she engineered my very existence?

But even as I asked myself the question, I suddenly remembered what Mr. Lange had said that day in his office—that his mother had kept a close eye on all the old families—that she probably knew about me before my own mother did. It was true. All of it. Mrs. Kane and those who believed in the curse might have been nuts, but the people running our side of things weren't playing with a full deck either.

I glared at her, hating her for what she'd done to my dad. To my mom. To my brother. To me. Even to Mr. Lange and Noelle and her mom. It was like she thought she was God. She couldn't mess with people's lives like that, and as soon as I had the chance, I was going to let her know how I felt about her.

As soon as I could get her away from my mother and Mr. Lange and my dad. Who might flatten her the same way he had Demetria Rosewell.

The crowd of officers on the other side of the room shifted, and one of them dragged a handcuffed Mrs. Kane out of a chair. Her makeup was smudged and her hair stuck out around her head as if she'd been hit with an electric shock. She kept her chin high as they led her across the room, but she trembled violently. Clearly she hadn't expected to end up this way. Clearly she'd had the utmost confidence in her crazy-ass plan.

Suddenly she turned to look at me, as if she'd felt me watching, and sneered. "This isn't over. You're trash and you will always be trash."

I felt a surge of anger and triumph all at once. I pulled away from my mother and Josh, even as they both tried to hold on to me, and strode toward her, my bare feet freezing on the cold cement floor. Clenching my teeth, I got right up in her face, ignoring the forbidding, outstretched arms of the police.

"At least I'm not going to prison," I seethed. "Have fun rotting in your prison cell with the rest of your crazy friends."

Mrs. Kane bared her teeth. Her eyes were like an abyss. Dark—so much darker than I'd ever realized. She let out a screech that couldn't have come from nature, and somehow flung the officer who was holding her to the floor.

Before anyone could move, she had freed herself from her handcuffs, grabbed a knife from the table where they were being bagged and tagged, and flung it, with both hands, at my chest.

"Reed!" Josh screamed.

"No . . . !" my father shouted.

But I couldn't move. As hard as I tried, I couldn't make myself move. It was as if I was being held in place by some invisible force. All I could do was think about how powerful Eliza Williams claimed I could be, and how very, very wrong she was if I couldn't even step aside to save my own life.

And then, out of nowhere, Mr. Lange flung himself in front of me. The knife pierced his chest with a sickening slicing sound I will never forget as long as I live. And just like that, Noelle's father, Theresa Billings's great-grandson, the person who'd given me life, fell to the floor at my feet. His eyes were open, his lungs were still.

I would never get the chance to thank him.

The PRIVATE series
KATE BRIAN

Welcome to Easton Academy, where secrets and lies
are all part of the curriculum . . . but these secrets
must be kept private whatever the cost.

Set in a world of exclusive boarding schools, Kate
Brian's compelling *Private* series combines the bitchy
snobbery of the elite and wealthy, with secrets,
mystery and satire. Dark, sinister and sexy
– with no parents around to spoil the fun . . .

CHARMING GIRLS.

FINE BREEDING.

PERFECT MANNERS.

BLACK MAGIC.

THE BILLINGS SCHOOL,

ESTABLISHED 1915,

WHERE THE GIRLS ARE WITCHES.

MEET THE ORIGINAL BILLINGS GIRLS IN